DEDICATION

For Jim.

My love, my heart, my best friend and my husband.

I love you.

The Hunter Bride

CYNTHIA WOOLF

ACKNOWLEDGMENTS

Many thanks to my editor Linda Carroll-Bradd, without whom I couldn't write this or any other book. Linda makes me work to bring out the best in my books.

Thanks also to my Just Write partners, Michele Callahan, Karen Docter and Cate Rowan. They always help me brainstorm and bring the story together.

Thanks to Romcon Custom Covers for my cover artwork.

CHAPTER 1

January 1872

Josephine "Jo" Shafter stood outside a small log cabin on the outskirts of Springfield, Illinois. She had hogtied Billy Jackson inside the shack and now waited for the sheriff to pick him up. She'd sent her man Jessup, to get the sheriff and bring him back here. Jackson would never kill anyone ever again. Her parents and little brother were finally avenged.

The unusually warm weather had melted the snow and turned the roads first to mud and now just dry and dusty. Jo swatted her hat back and forth across her thigh raising a cloud of dust. She didn't normally have to wrestle the fugitive quite so much, but Billy wouldn't go quietly and tried to overpower her, just because she was a girl. A lot of men made that mistake. Once. It wasn't easy being a bounty hunter, but she was one of the best, male or female.

Her father, the best bounty hunter she'd ever known, taught her everything she knew, including wrestling holds about which good ole' Billy hadn't a clue. She got his arm behind him, wrapped the rope around his wrist, pushed him to the ground and hooked the rope around his ankle, pulling tight so his ankle and wrists were next to each other and tied it off. He wasn't going anywhere.

Daddy also taught her how to shoot, hunt, and track just about any critter on two or four legs. He treated her as if she were a son. For the longest time she was the only child of Rex and Mary Shafter and hunted bounty's right along his side. Then Robby had come along. Jo was ten then and she remained the "son" until Robby turned ten.

At ten, Robby was old enough to learn to shoot, hunt, and track with her dad and her mother said the time had come for Jo to become skilled at being a wife. Though she still worked the occasional bounty, her mother taught Jo how to cook, a little anyway and bake, her biscuits were unrivaled.

The lessons hadn't advanced to sewing, cleaning, laundry and whatever else there was to learn. Her mother had died alongside Rex and Robby. Murdered by Billy Jackson and his gang. Jo's life changed that night. From then on she hunted, spent every waking minute searching for Jackson. Five years the task had taken her but she also had five years of other bounties she'd captured while waiting and searching for Billy Jackson. Five years of putting men wanted for every kind of act of violence and perversion behind bars where they couldn't hurt anyone again.

Yes, she'd become very good at her job and she had the bounty money to prove it. She'd collected his bounty, one thousand dollars even.

But the time had come to start anew. Time to get rid of the buckskins and put on a dress. Time to get married and start a family of her own. She was manlier than most of the men in town and they would never accept her as someone available to marry, not when she could best most of them at just about anything they did, from chopping wood to shooting and field dressing a deer.

Two months after she captured Jackson, Jo sat on the bench outside the courtroom and thought about what she'd do now. The solution had presented itself in the form of a newspaper ad for mail order brides. As she'd gotten close to capturing Jackson, she'd written to the address for the mail-order brides and ended up corresponding with Sam Longworth for about six months, or had it been nine. She closed her eyes and tried to remember. Oh well, the time didn't matter. Corresponding with him would have been very hard while she was on the trail, but Billy was dumb and kept circling back to what he knew, so she was able to send regular posts, a total of six letters to Sam.

He was the sheriff of a small mining town in the Montana Territory which was a good thing. She was familiar with his line of work and thought she should be safe from any of her former bounties showing up and wanting retribution.

She'd told him her family was killed in a carriage accident. Jo didn't want Sam to know that her family had been murdered. He might not want to marry her.

She stayed as close to the truth as possible, which made the lie easier to tell. Her family was killed but by Billy Jackson and his gang. He wanted revenge for her father taking in his brother. The brother had been hanged.

According to the police who investigated her family's murders, Jackson had gotten the drop on her father. He was found tied up across from her mother and little brother. Billy Jackson, the sick bastard, had forced her father to watch as he killed her mother and little brother. He'd killed her father last by slitting his throat. If she'd been home that night instead of out tracking a bounty, she'd have been killed, too. She knew if her father hadn't been able to save his family she couldn't have either.

Jo had made a promise to herself, to her family and to God, that she would find Jackson and his gang or die trying. She'd tracked them and she'd gotten all ten of the gang members. Now she finally had Billy. The last one. He'd been hard to find. Throwing his men to the wolves was nothing for Jackson. Every time she'd gotten close, he'd sent another of his gang members after her and every time she'd taken them in for the bounty. He'd finally gotten wise to that tactic and tried to take her in a ambush, but she and Jessup had killed everyone of the gang except Billy.

Finally, three months after the ambush she'd captured him. Jo stayed for the trial, heard him found guilty.

With all that behind her now, Jo could now think about the new life she was starting. In just two days she'd be boarding a west bound train from Chicago. She'd take it as far as Cheyenne and then ride the stage to Hope's Crossing in the Montana Territory. where she would meet her intended, Sheriff Sam Longworth. She hated having to lie to him, but she would become the kind of woman he wanted. Jo could learn to cook on a stove instead of a campfire.

She had a nice stash of money from her bounties and could hire out the laundry if need be. What if her new husband discovered she wasn't what he thought he was getting and he wanted to annul the marriage? All she had to do was have a wedding night but she wasn't sure she could do that. What if he didn't find her attractive enough to want a wedding night?

Jo wasn't *unattractive* with her golden hair and blue eyes. When she dressed as a woman, she'd been told she was quite appealing. She had a nice figure that didn't require a corset, which she was grateful for. Just the thought of donning that torture device sent chills up her spine. She'd gotten too used to the buckskin pants and coat along with her flannel shirts and boots that comprised her bounty hunter outfit to be comfortable in a dress, but she'd do what she had to. Sam was expecting a prim and proper young miss, and she would be one, even if it killed her.

*****

April 1, 1872, Hope's Crossing, Montana Territory

Sheriff Sam Longworth stood on the boardwalk outside the hotel and waited for the weekly stage. His bride was supposed to arrive on the noon coach. Of course, the stagecoach never arrived on time and a spring snowstorm had made traveling hard. He took his pocket watch from his vest pocket and checked the time. Half past two. This stage was later than usual, making him wonder if they'd run into Indian trouble in addition to the snow.

He looked down the long stretch of street, covered in snow. This was his town and he was proud of it, with its dirt streets, boardwalk, and white-washed single-story buildings, except the twelve saloons and six brothels, all of which were plain, unfinished wood and two-stories tall. Hope's Crossing Hotel was the jewel of town, three-stories in height, with windows in every room and glass in every window, glorious to behold.

Two miles south of town was Nevada City, an even smaller mining settlement. Together the two settlements had about 1200 residents, most of which were single men. Of the nineteen women in the two settlements, twelve of them were prostitutes. None were eligible, upstanding single women. Marrying women. That's why Sam had sent away for his bride.

There was one church, which didn't seem like a lot for the seven hundred or so people that lived there, but most of those inhabitants were miners and didn't attend services on a regular basis. They did, however, manage to keep him and his three deputies busy. His crew worked in shifts. He and Dave took the day shift and Tom and

Charley took the night shift.

"Stage's coming. Stage's coming."

Jamie Stone yelled the announcement like he did every week.

Sam put away his watch, straightened his hat, pulled on the lapels of his suit coat and then dropped his arms to his sides. He hadn't been this nervous since officer inspections when he first entered the army in 1861. When he left the army and became a bounty hunter, he'd gotten over such nerves, or so he thought until today.

He'd never told Jo he was a bounty hunter. His first wife left him because of his job, he didn't want the same thing to happen this time.

The coach pulled up to the wide boardwalk in front of the hotel where Sam stood. After the vehicle came to a stop, the shotgun rider, Bob Jones, climbed down and opened the stagecoach's door. Two men descended from the conveyance, followed by a woman with the prettiest blonde hair Sam had ever seen. She was the last person to get out.

Wally Smith, the stage driver lowered a large trunk to the shotgun rider, who set it up on the boardwalk, followed by two valises. Each of the men picked up one of the suitcases and entered the hotel.

The woman walked up the steps to where Sam waited. She lifted the skirt on her navy traveling suit to ascend the stairs, revealing riding boots, not dissimilar from his own. Frowning, he took a second look. The woman was actually wearing boots. He might have expected a lot of things, but this was not one of them. She dropped her skirt as soon as she reached the landing in front of the building and Sam wondered if he'd actually seen what he thought he did.

"Miss Shafter?"

"Yes. Sheriff Longworth, I presume."

He held out his hand. "Yes, ma'am, that's me."

Smiling, she took his outstretched hand and shook it.

Her hand felt so small in his, her skin rough from the gardening she said she did with the orphans.

"Please call me Jo."

"And I'm Sam."

She smiled. "Sam, do you have a room for me here at the hotel?"

"Actually, Jo," he ran his hand behind his neck. "I have the judge ready and waiting to marry us. We'll just drop your trunk off at my house on the way."

"Oh, my, I see."

She was quiet for a moment. "Very well, I suppose we should go."

I should have given her a church wedding or at least time enough to put on a clean dress.

Jo watched as he shouldered the trunk with ease and started down the boardwalk. A wagon rumbled past them down the dirt street, the horses kicking up dust with each step. Several people passed on the walk, all said hello to Sam, but none stopped.

Two blocks later they passed the sheriff's office and jail, a small one-story natural wood building with bars on the windows and the small window in the door as well. Sam's white wooden house was next door and he had a small barn in the back, which Jo thought unusual for a home in town. Sam dropped the trunk in the front room and then took Jo back outside.

"I see you have a barn. Does everyone here have a barn behind their house?"

"No. I do because I'm the sheriff and have to have access to a horse at all times. There is no telling when I'll have to go out after a criminal, it could be the middle of the night and I don't want to have to go down to the stable to find my animal."

"That makes sense."

"The judge's offices are a few more blocks. The mercantile is on the other side of the hotel where you got off the stage."

"How often so you go there?"

"Whenever I run out of something. I suppose you'll go on a more regular basis."

"I plan to."

The judge's offices were located in the only brick building in town. Jo recognized the building as a duplicate of the Cook County Courthouse's first floor. They went inside and found the chambers of Nathaniel Harden, according to the sign on the door.

Sam knocked once before entering.

"Nate? Are you here? We're ready to get married."

There was a shuffling sound from the back room and Nate Harden appeared wearing his black judge's robes. Nate was a rotund man about the same height as Jo, with a gray beard and hair.

"Who do we have here? Sam, will you introduce me?" asked the judge.

"Josephine   Shafter   this   is   Judge

Nate…er…Nathaniel Harden."

Jo held out her hand. "Pleased to meet you. Call me Jo."

Judge Harden took her hand.

"Nate just got back from Chicago where he observed the trial of some big time criminal, named Billy Jackson."

Jo's gaze snapped back to the judge who still held her hand.

Did he know? She'd only showed up for the first day of the trial. Just long enough to give her testimony about Billy's capture. She hadn't been there when her family was killed so couldn't testify about that. She'd left the state two days after that.

Nate cocked an eyebrow and smiled. "Pleased to meet you, Miss Shafter. "Shall we get this wedding started?"

Jo nodded. "Yes, sir. We should."

She retrieved her hand from the judge's. *He knew. He knew who she was.* She prayed he would not to say anything to Sam.

"All right, let me get the good book and we'll begin."

Jo let out a pent up breath. If he knew, he was keeping her secret.

"Now what are your full names?" The judge walked to the large dark wood desk, sat and got a pen and paper ready to jot down the replies.

"Josephine Elizabeth Shafter," replied Jo.

"Samuel James Longworth," said Sam.

The judge stood. "All right now, let's get this done and done. Do you Josephine Elizabeth Shafter take this man Samuel James Longworth…"

"I do," she replied at the proper time.

Sam placed a plain gold band on her finger.

He said the right words, too.

Jo put her father's ring on Sam's finger. Jackson hadn't taken the ring or any other jewelry or money. He'd only been interested in killing or had been interrupted, she didn't know which.

"I now pronounce you man and wife. You may kiss your bride."

Sam lifted her chin with his finger and then lowered his lips to hers. He gave her a nice…no…a very nice kiss.

When he stepped back, she touched her lips. Were they swollen as she felt they should be? That was her first ever real kiss from a man. Heavens to Betsy. If that was what she had to look forward to, she would be very happy wife.

*****

Hope's Crossing sat at the bottom of the foothills, surrounded on two sides by trees. The road from Bozeman cut through the middle of town and wound its way through a canyon to Nevada City.

After the ceremony they went back to Sam's house. Her house now, too. Once inside, he shut the door, turned and then pulled her to him.

"I've wanted to do this since I first saw you."

He lowered his head and pressed his lips against hers. Then his tongue pushed against her lips, silently pleading for entrance.

She granted it.

He surged forward engaging her tongue in sensual duel.

She dueled back—tasting, circling, playing.

He pulled away, smiling, and rested his forehead against hers.

"You please me, Jo. If I didn't have to work…" He sighed, "Ah, but I do. There's only four of us to take care of this entire town, otherwise we'd continue this right here and now. Besides I thought you might like to get settled in. I'll set your trunk in the bedroom. I emptied a couple of drawers in the bureau for you and made sure there's plenty of closet space. But if you need more, use the closet in the guest room."

"Thank you. I'm sure I'll be fine."

"I'll be home about six for dinner."

She nodded. "I'll do my best to have it ready by then."

"I'd give you a tour of the house but you've basically seen everything except the kitchen and you'll find that easily enough."

Her stomach tied itself in knots at the mention of dinner. Luckily her mother had taught her a few dishes and how to follow a recipe. She had two meals she could prepare without a written recipe. Then it was down to biscuits, bacon and eggs. She'd bought a cookbook called American Cookery before she left Chicago. Hopefully the recipes would not be too difficult.

Sam gave her another earth-shaking kiss, straightened and left down the hallway. His steps echoed off the wooden floor until they reached the carpeted living room, then silence and she heard the front door open and close.

She managed to get to the bed before her

knees gave out. Touching her fingers to her lips, they really did feel swollen from his kisses, but that wasn't possible…was it?

Sam was tall so she had to look up to him and that didn't happen very often, since at five foot ten inches she was very tall for a woman. He had golden brown hair and coffee brown eyes that could seduce her with just a look. She shook her head to get the fanciful thoughts out and get back to the task at hand.

First she changed out of her heavy blue traveling suit into a lighter weight dress. It was one of her favorites made from pale pink cotton and in a very simple shirtwaist style. Then Jo took a deep breath, rolled up her sleeves and walked to the trunk.

She decided she liked Sam's simple, but pleasant bedroom. The iron bed had a beautiful quilt of mostly blue and green material and two wooden nightstands stood on either side of the bed. Across the room was a six drawer bureau with mirror attached to the back. Next to it was the door to the closet. On the wall with the entrance door was a tall boy dresser and commode. On the wall opposite the door was a window which looked out into the back yard and was covered with blue calico curtains.

Curiosity got the better of her and she pulled out the drawers that held Sam's things. She figured she would find out soon enough what was in them when she put the laundry away, assuming she figured out how to do the washing.

The top drawer contained undershirts, the second long johns, the bottom had several pair of denims and one pair of buckskin pants. Buckskin? That was interesting. Did everyone here in Montana, wear buckskin pants?

The guest room was almost a duplicate, only the quilt gracing the bed was in shades of red and blue and the curtains were red calico.

She left her bounty-hunting clothes and pistols inside the steamer. No need for her handsome brown-eyed husband to see them and wonder what kind of woman he'd gotten for his bride.

After finishing with the trunk, Jo tied on one of her mother's aprons and explored the kitchen to see if his supplies included the ingredients for the chicken and dumplings she wanted to make. She opened the ice box and found a gallon of milk and at least two dozen eggs and one lowly chicken.

The meal she would make, one of the easiest dinners ever, her mother had said, required neither milk nor eggs.

She went over the recipe in her mind as she performed the tasks. Cut up a chicken as if for frying, and place in a Dutch oven and cover in water, season with salt, carrots and onions for flavor. She went to the sink and pumped the water. Thanks goodness she didn't have to go outside.

She let the chicken cook for several hours until the meat fell off the bone. Then she dropped biscuit dough by tablespoon into the boiling broth, covered the pan and let the dish cook for twenty minutes.

Jo made the mistake one time of peeking at the dumplings about half way through and they ended up with centers hard as rocks. She learned her lesson. Do not uncover until the twenty minutes are up and you remove it from the stove.

She found a can of peas in the pantry and opened those, made a pan of hot biscuits to go with the chicken dish and the meal was complete. She wondered if Sam would expect dessert. She wasn't much of a baker. When she'd gone through the pantry she remembered seeing a couple cans of fruit, peaches. That would make nice shortcake.

She was ready, now just to wait until Sam came home which wasn't as long as she thought.

Promptly at six, Sam came through the front door.

"Jo. I'm home," he called from the front room.

She took off the apron and placed it on the counter, then smoothed her skirt and hair before walking to the living room to greet her new husband.

What if he didn't like chicken? Or her biscuits? What would she do then? That's why he'd wanted a wife, to cook, clean and have children with. What if she wasn't up to the task?

CHAPTER 2

Sam took off his jacket and hung it, his hat and gun belt on pegs by the door.

He turned toward her as she entered the living room. "Mmm. Something smells good."

"I hope you like it." She stood with her hands clasped in front of her, her stomach full of butterflies.

He smiled. "I'll like anything that isn't my cooking."

"Good. I'll do my best. That's all I can promise."

"I'm sure it will be fine."

"I've got a basin in the kitchen for you to wash up and hot water on the stove."

"Thank you. It'll be nice to have the water ready for a change."

She followed him into the kitchen and while he washed she set the pot of chicken and dumplings on the table. Then she pulled the biscuits out of the warming shelf. They hadn't been in there very long so they were still hot. She set butter and what may have been chokecherry jam from the icebox on the table.

Sam sat. "This looks good. I don't know what it is though."

She handed him the serving spoon for the dumplings and a ladle for the gravy. "It's chicken and dumplings. Try it and tell me what you think. Take a bit of the chicken, a bit of the dumpling and the broth on your spoon."

He followed her instructions and rewarded her with a wide smile.

"This is great."

He grabbed a biscuit, buttered it and added some of the jam.

Now that she knew he approved, she relaxed some and settled down to eat her meal.

"So, how long was your trip?" Sam asked between bites.

"About a week. If the train came here, it would be a lot shorter."

"There's talk about that very thing, so moving the gold would be safer and easier but so far that's all it is. Talk."

"What about you," she said to Sam. "Tell me about Sam Longworth. There wasn't a lot we really said about each other in our letters. What are the things that you didn't write in the letters?"

"Not much. I like it here in Hope's Crossing. We're on the brink of big things, but we've already got laws in place so we can handle it."

"What's your favorite color?"

"Blue. Yours?"

"Purple or red. Sometimes purple is hard to find for clothes and such."

"What made you become a mail-order bride? I know your parents died five years ago, but you could have become a bride then. Why wait?"

How much of the truth can I tell him? "I was grieving. Trying to find a reason for their deaths. Until I could get over that portion of my life I couldn't move on."

"Have I told you how beautiful you are?"

She looked down at her plate, heat radiating from her cheeks.

"Thank you. That's very nice of you to say."

"You make it sound like you don't believe me, but you are Jo. I'm a lucky man."

"I'm a lucky woman. Your picture did not do you justice, but then the pictures never do. Everyone has to stand still for so long that they all look cranky, including you. I'm glad to see you can smile and have nice white teeth to show in that smile."

He laughed. "I wondered if you'd have any teeth, too. Something else we have in common."

"You're probably be sick of biscuits after this meal, but they are the one bread I'm good at making."

They ate in silence for a while. She got up and got the coffee from the stove.

"Would you like more?"

"Yes, please."

She filled his cup and then hers.

"I have peaches over biscuits for dessert."

"Another way to use biscuits? You certainly are inventive."

She served him the peaches with the juices from canning over the biscuit and topped it with the cream. Then she watched while he took a bite.

His eyes wide with surprise, he said, "This is good."

Thank God. He thinks I can cook. One less thing to worry about...at least until tomorrow night.

Sam dug into the dessert and finished it in no time. When he was done, he set his napkin on the table and patted his stomach.

"That was a wonderful meal, Jo."

"Thank you. I'm glad you liked it." She stood. "I'll get this cleared away, if you've had enough."

"I have. I'll read a bit before heading to bed."

"I'll be a few minutes. It won't take me long to clean up."

She cleared the table and covered the Dutch oven, putting the leftovers in the icebox. After washing and drying the dishes, she went to the living room.

Sam sat in one of the overstuffed chairs in front of the cold fireplace, reading by the light of a kerosene lamp on the table beside him. Next to him was a settee and at the other end of the sofa was another overstuffed chair. One day, Jo would rearrange the furniture, so the chairs were on one side of the table and the sofa on the other. It would allow more conversation when they had guests.

He looked up from his book. "All done?"

"Yes, I think I'll read a little while myself."

"Sure. Sit and relax."

"Let me get my book."

She walked down the hall to the bedroom to get her book from where she'd left it on the bureau. She lit the lamp by the bed, found her book and when she turned to leave she saw Sam leaning against the door frame, his lips turned up in a smile.

She held her book in one hand and the other hand at her throat. "Can I do something for you?"

"Yes, Jo, you can get undressed for bed. I find I'm not in the mood to read anymore tonight."

He pushed off the door and walked across to where she stood. "You are wearing entirely too many clothes."

Her heart pounded so hard she was sure he could hear it.

He unbuttoned her dress, slowly.

"I don't want to scare you. Tell me if I do."

She could barely breathe. Sam touching her was not exactly what she planned, but she did like it. "You're not scaring me."

Sam leaned down and kissed her, a gentle melding of their lips before he moved on to her neck behind her ear.

"Do you like this?" he whispered against her skin before his tongue followed his lips.

His moves left her skin on fire. "Y…y…yes," her voice cracked.

He opened her dress and slid it off her shoulders letting it fall to the floor.

"No corset?"

"Can't stand them, too restrictive," she breathed.

"A woman after my own heart."

Sam held her with his lips, feasting on hers as he walked her backwards to the bed. When her legs hit the mattress, she stumbled, but he caught her and lowered her back onto the quilt. Then he let go of her waist and trailed his fingers all the way down to her boots. He stopped and tugged each one off, and let it drop to the floor. She heard him slide her boots under the bed.

"Don't want to trip on those in the middle of the night."

Sam untied the ribbons holding up her

stockings, one at a time, and then worked the sock down her leg, his fingers tracing over her skin, making her shiver as he pulled the cotton off each foot and added them to the growing pile of clothes.

"Stand, please."

She followed his request and stood next to the bed.

He untied her chemise, pulling the ribbon free, opening the neckline wide down to her stomach and baring her breasts.

"There are the lovelies I'm after." He dropped his head to her breast and took one nipple into his mouth.

Jo gasped feeling more exposed than she ever had in her life. The cool air created goose flesh up and down her arms and across her stomach. Surprised and excited at the same time, she found herself without words.

"You are beautiful, Jo. Take off your chemise. Please"

Blood racing and knees shaking, she pulled it over her head and let it fall to the floor. "Now you have too many clothes on, Sam. It's time you undressed as well."

Jo had to do this. She had to make sure there would be no annulment. She wanted children and wanted this marriage. When Sam found out she'd cooked everything she knew how tonight and she didn't know how to do laundry or sew, she didn't want him to throw her back.

He shucked all his clothes in a snap and stood before her just as God had created him. Magnificent. His body was all hard angles and long muscles, and his shaft was wide and strong, ready for her.

"Now your bloomers." His voice was a low growl.

He breathed hard almost panted and his gaze never left hers.

She dropped them into the pile of clothes. Jo's mother had prepared her, she knew what came next. A little scared but more excited, she readied herself.

"Lie down on the bed," he ground out.

Jo lay down, her arms at her sides and her eyes closed.

She heard him chuckle.

"I'll do my best not to hurt you, but you need to relax."

She opened her eyes again. "You won't mean to, but you will hurt me. I'm not a child, I know how this works."

"Only the first time, and I'll prepare you

as much as I can."

She cocked her head and narrowed her eyes. "How?"

"Trust me. Will you do that? Just trust me."

She looked up into his caramel brown eyes, saw only concern for her there. Jo remembered their letters and the funny stories he shared of his childhood, of how much he missed his mother and nodded. "I trust you."

"Good."

He lay down beside her, propped on his left elbow. His right hand was busy touching her wherever he could reach. Over and around her breasts, then he tweaked her nipple and moved on. Again and again he moved, until finally he covered her nipple with his mouth and suckled her.

Gasping, she rose up, pushing her breast toward him.

He pressed his hand on her mound, slid a finger down to her special spot where he rubbed and sent her to the stars. "Sam." The anguished cry tore from her.

"That was…amazing." She caught her breath, feeling like she'd been running forever, totally spent.

"No more amazing than what comes next. Open your legs for me. Please, Jo."

She did as he asked and he fitted himself between her parted thighs pressing his member at her opening.

"I want you to relax. I'm doing my best not to hurt you."

"I know you are." She looked up into his warm brown eyes. "It's all right."

He pressed into her, slowly, at first, then he reared back and slammed through.

"Oh." She stiffened. The pain was minor, like getting a small cut on her finger.

He stilled. "Are you all right?"

She didn't answer for a moment, waiting for the pain to continue or even get worse, but the discomfort subsided.

"Jo? Did I hurt you? Are you in pain?"

"No. The pain in gone. Is there more?"

He began to breathe again. "Oh, thank God and yes, there is more."

Sam moved inside her, slowly, and then with more vigor. Finally he shouted and, after another pump or two, collapsed on her chest. He kissed her neck and then her lips.

"You were magnificent." He rolled off to the side.

She smiled. "And you are lying. I just

laid here while you did all the work."

"I expected that from you this first time. But tell me, how did you like making love?"

He pulled her in to cuddle with him.

She turned in his arms, pressing her breasts against his chest. Jo looked up at him and then smiled. "I guess it was all right. The first part I like much better than the second."

He laughed. "As you should…this time. For me the second part is the best. From now on there will be no more pain, so you'll like the second part better, too. I promise. We have a lot of years to learn each other's needs and desires. For now let's just sleep."

She didn't think she could sleep. Images of the day worked their way into her consciousness. Traveling, the wedding, unpacking, dinner and then making love. This is what she wanted. Home, husband and children. So why wasn't she happier?

Could the reason be that she already missed her old life? The danger, the thrill of the hunt and then the satisfaction of putting another piece of scum behind bars. Or was she dreading the day in the not-too-distant future when her husband found out she wasn't who he thought she was?

*****

Sunlight shone through the blue curtains. Jo couldn't believe she'd slept so late. The sun was already up. Usually she was up long before daybreak. She stretched, remembered where she was and realized there was no breathing coming from that side of the bed. She glanced at the mattress next to her. It was empty. The wonderful smell of hot coffee assaulted her senses and she turned toward the door.

"Miss me?"

Sam stood in the doorway with only his pants on, holding two cups of coffee, the delicious aroma having reached her nose before he entered the room.

She sat up, pulling the sheet to cover her breasts and held out her hand. "Oh, please. I need coffee."

He smiled, walked to the bed and handed her one of the cups.

She sipped the hot liquid and closed her eyes. "Mmm. Good. Coffee gets me going in the mornings. It's late though. I never sleep this late. Why didn't you wake me?"

"You had a big day yesterday." He waggled his eyebrows. "I wanted to let you sleep in a little today."

"I need to fix breakfast. Will you turn your back so I can get dressed?"

He shook his head.

"Might as well get used to it. I like looking at you naked. Or dressed. I just like looking at you. You're a beautiful woman, Jo."

"Fine." She threw back the blankets, plucked yesterday's chemise and bloomers off the floor by the bed and went to the commode where the pitcher and basin were. She quickly washed her feminine parts and her underarms and then put her under clothes on. Then she walked to the closet picked out a pink blouse and black bombazine skirt. She donned both pieces of clothing all the while staring back at Sam. Last she walked back to the bed, rolled on her stockings, tied them in place with a ribbon around her thigh and shoved her feet in her boots before dropping her skirt back in place.

Sam leaned against the door frame with his arms crossed across his chest and a silly grin on his face. He definitely enjoyed the show.

"Do you normally get up earlier?" She tucked her blouse into the waistband of her skirt.

"Yes, I have a cow and two goats to milk, eggs to gather and chickens to feed. I also have a billy goat and a donkey, all of which live in the barn and have to be fed. Well, except for the chickens. They're in the chicken coop."

"Why don't you get the milk and eggs from the store? You'd save yourself a lot of time in the mornings."

"And spend a lot of money that I don't have. Besides Snyder's Mercantile doesn't carry milk and the eggs they get are usually already sold before the delivery even comes into the store. You'll be doing the milking and egg gathering from now on."

She shook her head, buttoning her cuffs as she and walked toward him. "I don't know how to milk a cow or goat or deal with chickens. We bought all of that at the market back home." Jo walked past him out into the hall turned and waited for him.

He pulled a clean shirt off a hanger and put it on. "Well then you have some new things to learn. Tomorrow I'll take you out and teach you how to gather eggs and milk both the goat and the cow. They are similar but different."

"How many chickens do you have?"

"Ten that I keep for cooking and twelve that are laying hens."

"Do you get a dozen eggs every day?" She started walking down the hall.

Sam followed her, as he rolled up his cuffs. "Yup."

"What do you do with that many eggs every day? Surely you don't eat them all?"

"I usually sell half."

"That explains why you have so many eggs in the icebox."

"Yes, but now that you're here we'll use them faster. You'll use them in recipes and for baking as well as cooking."

Guilt stabbed her. She looked down and checked the buttons on her cuffs again. "Yes, we'll use them when I do all that cooking. I'm making biscuits with sausage gravy for breakfast this morning. I'll fix you a couple of eggs as well."

Sam rubbed his hands together. "I can't wait to have some real home cooking. My pitiful attempts kept hunger away but can't be called good."

Jo swallowed hard. "What were you doing with the sausage?"

"Fry it up in patties. I can handle

breakfast eggs, meat and bread, but after that, I'm terrible. First I don't know what to cook and second I don't know how to cook whatever I decide on unless it's breakfast."

"We'll have to see if I can do better." She had better get the cookbook out of her trunk and get busy reading recipes and finding ingredients.

She left Sam to finish dressing, and headed to the kitchen. She crumbled the sausage and put it on the stove to fry. Then she stirred together another batch of biscuits and put them in the oven. Once the sausage was cooked Jo scooped out the meat, made gravy with the drippings and added back the meat. She pulled the biscuits out of the oven and put them on the warming shelf. Last, she melted butter in another skillet and fried three eggs, just for Sam. The man couldn't say he left the table hungry.

He sat at the table and began to eat. "This is good."

She swallowed. "Thank you. I'm glad my paltry efforts are pleasing you."

"I think you're doing just dandy."

Her cheeks heated under his praise and she looked down at her plate but not without a smile.

Sam's fork clattered on his empty plate. "Fine meal, Jo. Fine meal."

She took the dishes to the sink. "I'm glad you liked it."

He walked over and gave her a kiss on the cheek. "See you at lunch time. What will you bring over to the jail?"

"Over to the jail?" He expected her to bring him the midday meal?

"Yeah, you'll have to bring it to me. My deputy is on rounds at that time."

"The jail is right next door, why can't you come home? Do you actually have anyone incarcerated?"

"Well, no, but…"

"Then you can close your office and come home for lunch." She paused, realized her bounty hunter self was coming out and softens her voice. "And by the way, if you want to eat any more chicken you better butcher it. I don't know how and I don't intend to learn."

He frowned. "You wrote you could cook anything?"

"That's right, cooking not butchering. I got my chickens from the butcher, all ready for cooking." Guilt washed over her. She had said in her letters, she could cook anything. Cook it not butcher it. But even the cooking part was a stretch.

He scratched his head. "All right, I can kill them and prepare them for cooking but it's probably just easier if you go to the butcher. He's a few doors down from the hotel where you arrived. If you bring me my lunch, we can eat together and then I'll take you around to the merchants and introduce you."

"You're a devious man, sheriff, figuring a way to get me to bring your food to you. Well, just for today."

He grinned. "We'll see."

A knock sounded on the front door.

Sam walked out to the answer the door, and Jo followed.

The knock sounded again.

"I'm coming. Hold your horses." He opened the door. "What?"

An older man probably about fifty, stood on the porch. "Sorry, to get you out so early, sheriff, but there's trouble down at the Branch."

Sam took his gun belt off the peg by the door, checked the load in the pistol's chamber and buckled it around his waist before turning to Jo. "See you later." He nodded and walked out the door.

What kind of trouble was at the Branch? What was the Branch? A saloon?

CHAPTER 3

Jo watched Sam leave with the man and wondered what kind of trouble there had been at the Branch, which she assumed was a saloon but it could have been the bank branch. *No.* She admonished herself. *You don't go after bounties any longer. Just because you found most of yours inside a saloon, doesn't mean there are any wanted men killing time in watering holes here.*

Frustrated that she didn't know what businesses were in town and whether the Branch was a saloon or a bank, she closed the door a little harder than she needed to. She returned to the kitchen and finished cleaning up. Then she found the cookbook and started reading recipes. As long as she had this cookbook she'd be all right in the cooking department. She trusted that she would be anyway. Sewing and keeping house were different problems. She couldn't sew a lick and thought she'd be fine cleaning as long as he didn't want it perfect. She was basically a neat person, tossing her clothes on the floor last night notwithstanding. If Sam wasn't well, she'd teach him to be.

After nodding off more than once while reading the cookbook, she decided she'd just prepare leftovers for lunch. She could do something else after visiting the butcher. And she wanted Sam to take her to get the mail. She was expecting a letter from the Cook County Courthouse confirming Billy Jackson was delivered to prison or being hung. She knew the mail came in on the stage because she'd seen the mail pouch when the driver had unloaded her trunk.

She marked several recipes in the book, made the bed, and did the dishes. But her curiosity was getting the better of her. She couldn't wait to find out what happened at the Branch, decided to take Sam his lunch, a little early. She heated up the chicken and dumplings, gathered plates, utensils into a flour sack, wrapped biscuits in a dish towel, placed those in the sack, too and carried the sack and the cast iron Dutch oven over to the jail.

"I'm here," she said when she entered the building.

Sam was behind his desk, stood to greet her and then sat again. "Ah, good. You can meet my deputy. Jo Longworth this is Dave Mosley."

He was the same man from this morning. He had graying hair and a slight paunch. "Pleased to meet you, Mr. Mosley."

"And I you, Mrs. Longworth. 'Fraid I couldn't stay this morning, not with Buffalo Barney raisin' a ruckus down at the Branch."

Though she was sure she knew the answer, she asked anyway. "What is the Branch?" She set the pot of food on top of the pot-bellied stove in the corner.

"The Branch Water Saloon. It's one of the livelier saloons in town. We've got fifteen saloons, five brothels, and one church, but we hardly ever have a problem at the church."

Dave chuckled at his jest then ducked his head and blushed.

"Sorry to be rattlin' on so."

"Nonsense. I love hearing all the ins and outs of the town." Jo assured him. She wanted to make a friend of Dave Mosley.

"What kind of problem was Mr. Buffalo causing?"

Shaking his head, Sam laughed. "It's not Mr. Buffalo. It's just Buffalo or Barney. He's only both names in his stories, and he can tell some doozies."

Jo shooed Sam's boots off the desk and set the sack of dishes where they had been. "There is plenty of food for both of you. Biscuits are in the sack and the chicken and dumplings are on the stove."

"Wow, hot food. We ain't had a hot midday meal in ages." Dave grabbed a plate and silverware and filled his plate with the succulent offering.

"Where would I go to get the mail?" Jo looked down and played with the strings to her reticule.

"That would be the Hope's Crossing Hotel, where you got off of the stagecoach. Are you expecting something?" asked Sam, his fork held suspended in front of his mouth.

"Not really. Just a letter from some friends. Given as long as it took me to get to Montana Territory, I figure any letters probably beat me here."

She wasn't about to tell him she was waiting for confirmation that Billy Jackson either went to prison or was hung for killing her family. She hadn't stayed for the sentencing.

"Well, as long as you are both happy with your lunch, I'll go see if there is any mail for me."

"I'll see you after work." Sam walked over and gave her a kiss on the cheek. "If we were alone," he whispered, his dark gaze connecting with hers. "I'd give you much more than a kiss."

"Oh, my." Heat rose in her cheeks. She imagined him kissing her like he did last night and suddenly she felt hot all over. "I better go."

Sam laughed and squeezed her shoulders before releasing her.

Jo walked out the door and then to the hotel where an elderly woman sat behind the counter.

"What can I do for you, dearie?"

"I came to see if any mail has been delivered for me. I'm Jo Longworth. The sheriff and I just got married, but the mail probably came to Jo or Josephine Shafter."

"I'm Iphigenia Smith, but they call me Effie." She slipped off the stool she was sitting on and turned to the cubbyholes behind her. She rattled on, "I run the hotel, the bath house and the post office. I had to sell the general store to my sister. Just couldn't run everything by myself. Couldn't give her more than the mercantile 'cause she's a little older than me. She's seventy-two now, I'm only sixty-eight, but there's just so many hours in the day."

Jo smiled at the little gray-haired woman. She was very short, the top of her head only hit Jo at mid-chest, and wore a pink seersucker dress with white lace trim. She'd pulled her silver-gray hair up into a bun on top of her head. Jo thought she was just the cutest little lady she'd ever met, reminding Jo of her grandmother.

"Now, let's see here what we have in the mail."

She looked in the slots behind her that Jo had originally thought were for the rooms.

"I have one here for Josephine Shafter

from the Cook County Court in the State of Illinois. I think that is probably for you."

Relief coursed through her. Finally the case was done. "Yes ma'am. I've been waiting to hear on a particular case."

Effie handed her the envelope.

Jo ran her finger along the flap on the letter and pulled out the sheet of paper. It was from the Clerk of the Court.

Dear Miss Shafter:

Mr. William Jackson was sentenced to death by hanging for the murders of Rex, Mary and Robert Shafter. I am sorry to inform you he was en route to the penitentiary when the vehicle was stopped and all the prisoners set free. The escape plan was to release another prisoner, Frank Bauer, but the idea to release all of them aided in the escape of Bauer.

All of the other prisoners except William Jackson and Frank Bauer have been recaptured.

We believe that Mr. Jackson and Mr. Bauer are traveling together and are headed in the direction of the Montana Territory and Hope's Crossing. Mr. Jackson spoke more than once about "getting even" with you for his incarceration.

We advise you to be on guard at all times and to inform your local law enforcement of the probable appearance of Jackson and Bauer in the area.

Sincerely,

John D. Ratcliff, Clerk of Cook County Courts

"Damn!" Jo said before she remembered where she was. "Forgive my language, Effie."

"Bad news, dearie?"

"Unexpected news, but I'll take care of it. Thank you, Effie."

"Anytime. Anytime at all."

Anger coursed through her. So much so, her hand shook as she shoved the letter back in the envelope and tucked it into her reticule. Jo stalked back home and then tried to search the cookbook for a dinner recipe, but all she could picture was Billy Jackson standing over the bodies of her family.

"Damn! Damn! Damn!" She slammed the book closed and sat at the kitchen table with her head in her hands. Just as she was getting her life started, she had to be wary of him sticking up his nasty red-haired head. The next time she caught him—and she would—she'd make sure he hung. She'd stay and see it done, if she had to do it herself.

For now though, what would she tell Sam? She had to tell him something because she would eventually be leaving...or would she? Maybe she could track Jackson while still tending to other duties. How hard could accomplishing that be? Depending on how far off the beaten track he rode to follow her, he could already be there. Somewhere. The town wasn't that big. She'd find him or her name wasn't Josephine Elizabeth Longworth.

*****

Several evenings and two new recipes later, after they had finished dinner, she and Sam sat in the living room reading. She liked to read romance novels and Sam liked adventure novels. Jo supposed she ought to learn how to knit or crochet or something, but she really preferred to read.

"Are you ready for bed?" Sam waggled his eyebrows at her.

The man was insatiable. Of course, she had to admit, the act of making love was a lot more pleasant the second, third, and fourth times.

She grinned. "I'm always ready for

you."

He stood and hauled her out of the overstuffed chair in front of the fireplace. Then, he bent and put her over his shoulder, gave her a swat on the butt, and they both laughed on the way to the bedroom.

Tonight, she would tell him. She had to. Jackson could be out there, waiting for her, and she needed to be ready.

When they got to the bedroom she set her feet on the floor.

Then he began to unbutton his shirt.

"You're slow getting undressed tonight, Jo."

She was slow, trying to find a way to tell her husband she was nothing like he thought was a difficult task.

"Sam?"

"Hmm?" He sat on the bed taking off his boots.

"What if I couldn't do all the things you want me to or that you think I can do?"

"Like what?"

She stood with her back to him, fingers on her buttons. "Oh, like cook and clean and sew."

"Seems to me you already are doing those things. So it wouldn't matter if you say you can't, because you already do. Understand?"

She thought about what he said and realized he was right. Except for sewing, she *was* doing everything he expected.

"Have you gotten any new wanted posters lately?" She removed her blouse and skirt, then her bloomers. Her chemise, which went down to her knees, she left on until last. Tonight, she planned on teasing him.

"Why would you care about the posters that came in?" He removed his boots and pants, but left on his under drawers.

"I just do." She should probably tone down her interest. "I…um…find it interesting to see what kinds of crimes these people come up with." She turned and started to unlace her chemise while sashaying over to where he stood next to the bed.

"We did get one in that you might be interested in. One for Billy Jackson, that man whose trial Nate went to in Chicago. We got a new poster on him. He's escaped from prison."

Jo went still. He knew about Jackson. Had he gotten a letter from the County Clerk like she did?

None of that mattered right now. She wanted her husband and certainly didn't want him to know she had more than just a passing interest in Billy Jackson.

He dropped his drawers.

She sucked in a breath. Her body ached for him, moisture already flowing to her center. But she was determined.

Sam came toward her but she danced out of his reach.

He stopped, cocked an eyebrow and crossed his arms over his chest.

Jo unlaced her chemise, completely removing the ribbon. She danced around Sam, trailing the ribbon over his arms and shoulders. Each time he reached for her she twirled away only to return with the ribbon.

Suddenly Sam picked her up and took her to the bed. She thought he must have had enough of the teasing. He laid her gently on the bed, then came down over her, his lips meeting hers and plying them with nips and caresses, but never letting them go.

She wrapped her legs around him.

"Ahh," she sighed as he entered her.

"You are ready for me." He rocked against her.

"I'm always prepared for you." She

moved her hands over his back, digging in her nails as he relieved the ache she felt deep inside her.

After he took them both to heaven and back, he pulled her close for a cuddle. Wrapped in the warmth and safety of his arms, she hated that she had to deceive him, but he would never understand that she was a bounty hunter, not when he wanted a demure wife. He'd been specific and she'd answered because she thought she could be that person. She thought she was done with bounties, but she couldn't be done hunting until Jackson was hanged.

*****

The next morning, Sam left for the day just after breakfast.

As soon as he was gone, Jo went to her trunk and took out her gun and holster. She put it on over her dress and then pulled on her winter coat to hide the rig. Next she walked up to the hotel to talk to Effie.

"Well, hello there, Jo."

Effie stood behind the registration desk. As Jo drew closer she saw that she was sorting mail.

"Hello, Effie. Was the stagecoach early today?"

"Oh, no." She shook her head. "This is yesterday's mail."

"I see. Say Effie, have you seen a man in here about my height with red hair and a beard. He also has the greenest eyes I've ever seen."

"Why, yes, dearie. He was in here the day after you arrived, the same day you came to get the mail. He asked after you, and I sent him in your direction." She frowned. "Didn't he find you?"

"No." Her stomach did a flip. "He didn't." Damn. He knew where she lived which meant he also knew that she was married to the sheriff. What would that force Jackson and anyone else with him, to do? "Thank you, Effie."

"Anytime, honey. You take care of that handsome Sam for me."

"I'll do my best." Jo smiled at the little woman. "See you later."

Jackson had been in Hope's Crossing for nearly two weeks, and she hadn't seen hide nor hair of him. She should tell Sam. Her guilt told her she should tell Sam, but first she wanted to know what Jackson was waiting for.

Jo ran back to the house, ignoring the

stares of the people on the boardwalk. When she reached home she took out one of her Colts and searched all around the perimeter, looking for some sign that Jackson had been there. When she reached the kitchen side of the house, she found boot tracks under the window. When had he watched her? For how long? And where did he go after?

CHAPTER 4

Jo followed the tracks to the livery stables. She walked into the barn-like structure and saw the owner working over a hot fire and anvil, forming a horseshoe with a hammer.

"Mr. Jenkins."

Clang!

"Mr. Jenkins!"

Clang!

"Mr. Jenkins!" she yelled it as loud as she could.

"Oh, Jo." He lay down the hammer and stuck the horseshoe into the fire. "Did you convince that husband of yours that you need a horse of your own?"

She shook her head, agitated that she needed to participate in small talk. "Unfortunately, not yet, but I'm not deterred. Actually, I came to ask about someone else. Have you seen a man about my height with red hair and a beard? He'd be looking to buy a horse and rig."

"I had someone like that in about a week ago. Didn't have much money, but I had a decent horse to sell. He was a fine looking paint. You can't miss him with those white and black markings. Not another horse like him in the area."

"Thanks for the information, Mr. Jenkins." She waved her hand at the stalls. "Are you still holding that big chestnut stallion with the white socks for me?"

"Yes, ma'am," He took off his work gloves and shoved them in his pocket. "But I don't know how long I'll be able to. I got lots of people wanting to buy him."

"I promise that I'll be by tomorrow to pick him up." She grinned. "I'll tell Sam it's a wedding present."

"That ought to do it."

"Thanks again. I better get home and start supper. Sam will be home before I know it."

"Yes ma'am the sun will be setting in less than an hour."

She raised her eyebrows. "What time is it?"

He took a watch from his pocket and flipped it open.

"It's half past four."

Jo stamped her foot. "Darn where did the day go? I always lose track of the time at sundown because of these mountains. See you tomorrow." She ran from the stable across town to her home. Sam would be home in less than ninety minutes and she was supposed to have a roast cooking.

When she reached home, Jo took off her gun and stashed it back in the trunk. Then she threw on an apron and took the beef from the icebox. Next she heated a skillet on the stove and seared the roast until it was good and brown all over, then she put it in the oven.

One of the nice ladies in town had canned green beans with potatoes and bacon and given several jars to Sam. Jo didn't want to know why the woman gave Sam the food. She figured the lady was trying to garner favor with the handsome, and at that time, eligible sheriff. Ignoring her thoughts, she set the Dutch oven on the stove, dumped two quarts of the vegetables into the pan and started the food to heat.

Jo took a table cloth from one of the kitchen drawers and covered the kitchen table with it. She hadn't used the table cloth before and maybe if she set an especially nice table, Sam wouldn't notice the food. She set the dishes and silverware for two and went back to the stove. She didn't have time to make biscuits, so she took the loaf she bought at the bakery out of the breadbox and left it on the cutting board ready to slice.

"Jo," Sam called from the living room. "I'm home."

She went to meet him, untying her apron as she walked.

"Hello, did you have a good day?" she asked without looking up. When she finished getting her apron loose she glanced up to see that Deputy Mosley accompanied Sam. "Well, hello Dave. Are you joining us for dinner?"

"Yes, ma'am, Jo. Hope you don't mind."

"Not at all. You're always welcome here."

Sam rubbed his hands together. "What did you fix?"

"A beef roast."

"Sounds good. Are you ready for us?" asked Sam.

"Why don't you and Dave get seated while I get another place setting?"

The men followed her into the kitchen and sat at the square wooden table. Jo grabbed another plate and set of silverware and placed it on Sam's left. Then she went back to the stove and opened the oven. The delicious smell from the roasting meat permeated the room with a wonderful aroma. Could she be lucky enough to have a cooked roast in just the half hour it had been in?

Taking the potholders from the top of the warming shelf, Jo pulled the roast out of the oven.

"Smells great, Jo. Do you need any help?" asked Sam.

"No, I'm fine. Be right there." She took the largest knife and sliced the end piece of meat. It didn't look too bad. The second slice was terrible. It was raw. Not rare, but almost totally raw. She glanced over her shoulder and saw the expectant faces of Sam and Dave and decided to go ahead and serve the meat. Maybe they liked it rare. There was a little browning where she'd seared it, but it needed another hour in the oven to be anywhere near cooked. She sliced another piece and then took the plate to the table.

Sam's smile faded and his eyes widened. He looked at Dave, whose expression was much the same.

The men smiled at her and each took a piece of meat.

She retrieved the green beans and potatoes from the stove, poured them into a large serving bowl, and then she sliced the bread and placed the slices on a long serving plate with the crock of butter.

Jo sat after getting dinner on the table and took the end piece of meat which was at least edible. She was totally embarrassed by the meal, but determined to prove to herself she could look for Jackson and still be a good wife to Sam. So far her plan was not working.

Sam and Dave looked at each other and bravely cut a piece of their roast, put it in their mouths and chewed. Swallowing quickly. Each of them took a large portion of the beans and potato dish and two slices of bread.

Jo watched in horror as they continued

to eat the raw meat.

Finally, she rose and took a skillet from the hooks on the wall behind the stove and set it on the burner. Without a word she took the roast off the table and cut two thick slices into the sizzling hot skillet, frying them on each side until good and brown.

When the roast slices, which were now steaks, were cooked she took them to the table and switched them with the raw meat on the plates of the men.

"I'm sorry," she serving them the steaks. "You are both so kind not to say anything. I let the day get away from me and didn't get the roast in the oven on time. It looks like we're having steak tonight and roast tomorrow. Forgive me?"

Sam smiled. "I'm just relieved you realized the thing wasn't cooked. I don't know how long I could have kept up the pretense of enjoying it."

"Dave, if you come back tomorrow, you'll have a fine supper of properly prepared food. I promise."

The deputy grinned. "I appreciate the offer, Jo. If you'd made it without admitting that this was not cooked right, I wouldn't be back in a million years. But I believe I will take you up on the invitation now."

Jo laughed. "You should have seen your faces. The look of horror when you saw the meat was priceless."

The two men laughed, but the sound was weak, like they weren't sure the situation was really all that funny.

Their response made Jo laugh even more.

Finally, the men retired to the living room while Jo cleaned up the kitchen. A few minutes later, Sam walked up behind her and wrapped his arms around her waist.

"You know I'll pay you back for dinner tonight," he whispered in her ear before kissing her neck.

"Has Dave left?"

"Yes. We're alone."

She loved when he made her pay for some supposed infraction of their marriage agreement. Tonight would be the one where she'd said she would prepare a proper meal. She will have deserved every little lick and caress he made her endure while he took his sweet time sending her to oblivion.

Oh, yes, she looked forward to tonight's play.

"I know. I've been a very bad girl."

"Yes, you have. Very bad. How about you finish those later?" He pointed toward the sink full of dishes.

"Only if you help. I'll wash and you dry."

"Deal."

She snatched a dry dish towel from the drawer to the left of the sink and dried her hands.

"Ready when you are." She took his hand and pulled him after her as she hurried to the bedroom.

"I'd say you're more ready than I am." He chuckled behind her.

"It's been a hectic day, I need some relief."

He slipped his arms around her when they reached the bedroom.

"What was so hectic?"

"Well, I went to Effie's and visited with her, and then I went to the stables and assured Mr. Jenkins that I would be by to purchase that chestnut stallion. Please Sam, let me have him. I'll buy him myself, but please say yes."

Sam frowned. "What do you mean you'll buy him yourself?"

Jo slapped her hand across her mouth,

and then removed it with a sigh. "I should have told to as soon as we married, but I was scared and didn't know what kind of man you were. Not really. You could have been the opposite of what you wrote. Anyway, I have money left to me by my parents and my grandmother." The lie rolled off her tongue with ease. How could she tell him she'd earned the money as a bounty hunter? He would feel emasculated and divorce her. Every man she'd ever encountered was intimidated by her because of her job.

"How much money are we talking about?"

"About eight thousand dollars. I intended to tell you, but the existence just slipped my mind. I'm truly sorry Sam."

His arms slipped from around her and he walked away.

She followed him back to the living room.

"No, don't be sorry. I understand your reasoning, and I might have done the same thing if I were you." He ran his hand around the back of his neck. "As to forgetting about it, well, where is this money? In the bank?"

Relief coursed through her. He wasn't angry about the money. She nodded. "I had it wired to the bank here when I was sure I was coming. We need to appear there together to have it transferred to your account…except for the amount for my horse, Checkers."

"Checkers?" His eyebrows shot up. "You've already named the horse?"

"I knew my husband wouldn't keep something from me that I want so much. A hundred dollars is not really a lot of money for the animal. He's got good strong lines and all his teeth, I checked. Please come see him and then, if you really don't want me to have him, I won't ask again."

"All right. We'll go look at this stallion tomorrow."

He kept his back to her.

She couldn't see his face.

"Sam?" She put her arms around his waist and lay her cheek against his back. "Thank you. Now come to bed."

He patted one of the hands on his waist and slipped out of her arms as he turned toward her.

"Go to bed, Jo. I'm staying up for a while."

She knew she'd hurt him, but she was only looking out for herself. There was no telling what kind of man Sam was before they met but when she'd decided he was a good man, she should have told him about the money. Or at least when she found the horse she wanted at the livery, she should have told him. But she didn't and now she would pay the price. After dragging herself down the hallway, Jo lit the lamp, dressed for bed, lay down on her side and cried, sad she'd been the cause of their first argument.

During the night she woke and found herself in Sam's arms with the lamp still burning.

"What? I thought you were mad at me." She sniffled, tears still filling her eyes.

"You were crying in your sleep. I don't want you to cry, Jo. It just tears me apart to see you so unhappy."

"Oh, Sam." She slid her fingers along his jaw. "I'm so sorry. Truly I am."

He adjusted his arm and pressed her head against his shoulder.

"I'm the one who's sorry. Keeping your money was perfectly reasonable until you were sure about me. I was hurt by the fact that after four weeks, you still aren't sure of me."

"That's not true. I knew you were a

good man the day you married me. And then you kissed me, opened yourself for me. I knew and, truly, if I had remembered about the money I would have told you. I only thought about it today because of the horse. I want to buy the horse, Sam. Please tell me I can."

She bit her tongue wanting to tell him she'd spend her money how she saw fit, but that wasn't the way of the world. If she wanted to be married and have children, she had to defer to her husband. She knew this but that didn't stop it from grating on her.

"Does having that horse mean that much to you? You could use the donkey for anything you need."

"I want my own horse, Sam. A horse not a donkey. It means the world to me. I can go do things without bothering you. If I want to go and pick wild blueberries in the forest, I can and I do happen to know where some are. Miss Effie told me. I can make pancakes or muffins with them, or even a pie, if you want. I have a recipe for cherry pie," she walked her fingers up his chest. "That will probably work for blueberries."

"Jo."

"Yes, Sam?"

"You're rambling." He bent his head, found her lips and kissed her quiet.

When he broke the kiss she was breathless, as usual.

"How do you do that? Kiss me, and I forget everything I was thinking. I only know the kiss and you."

He pulled her on top of him and looked into her eyes.

"Because I fill your senses, as you do mine. You're not the only one affected by our kisses. They are special, Jo, just as you are."

"Oh, Sam," She rubbed her hand along his jaw. "You know what to say to a girl."

"Only this girl."

"Kiss me again, please."

"With pleasure, sweet wife."

Jo couldn't figure out why she was so upset that she had disappointed Sam. Tears filled her eyes and she knew. Guilt. That's why she was upset. She'd lied to him about other things but this seemed more personal. Or would she have the same reaction when he found out how she really got the money? She didn't like lying to Sam. Not at all.

CHAPTER 5

The next morning, Jo and Sam walked down to the stable.

The streets were bustling with people and vehicles. Wagons in from the mine for supplies. Farmers dropping off their goods at the mercantile. The weather, though sunny, was cool enough that Jo tucked her hands around the crook in Sam's elbow for warmth. Ladies young and old, tittered behind their gloves when Sam passed. That fact that Jo was walking with him didn't matter at all to some of the more brazen women.

"Hello, Sam," said a brunette with lovely skin and pretty blue eyes.

"Hello, Emily. Have you met my wife, Jo?" He turned to Jo. "My dear, this is Emily Dodge. She is the bank president's daughter."

Jo extended her right hand keeping her left firmly around Sam's arm.

"Pleased to meet you *Miss* Dodge."

The young woman didn't want to, but shook Jo's hand, dropping it almost before she took it.

They walked by a couple of saloons including the Branch Water. Tinny piano music came from inside. Jo tried to peer through the glass window in the door, but it was so dirty she couldn't see anything and Sam pulled her away.

Finally they reached the livery stable.

"Hello, Mr. Jenkins," Jo called as they entered the barn looking building, waiting for the gray haired, bearded man to answer.

"Well, hello there, young lady." Jenkins walked out of one of the stalls carrying a pitchfork and wearing a pair of overalls with a plaid flannel shirt. "I see you brought our sheriff with you. Hello, Sam."

"Paul." Sam placed his arm around Jo's waist. "The little wife here wants a horse of her own and says you have the animal she's set her heart on. A big chestnut stallion she's already named Checkers."

"I don't know nothin' about any name. The folks that sold him to me called him Smokey."

Immediately the horse nickered.

"Well," Jo sighed. "I guess we have a horse named Smokey, since he already knows his name. Do you have a rig for him?"

"Yup." Paul Jenkins walked over to the rail on the first stall which was empty. "It's a good set, too. Practically new and a bargain at twenty-five bucks."

"Paul." Sam looked at the bridle and checked the straps on the saddle. "If you're talking about this saddle, you know it's only worth twenty dollars and needs new straps thrown in." He pulled on the leather girth strap attached to the shiny black saddle.

Jo saw it give and knew Sam was right. The straps needed replacing.

Mr. Jenkins raised his hands in surrender. "All right, you got a deal on the rig, with new straps all around, bridle, too. But the horse is eighty-five dollars and not a penny less."

Jo walked with Sam to the stall of the

horse in question. He was a true chestnut, reddish brown hair and not a trace of black. Even his eyelashes were brown. He was tall, a good seventeen or eighteen hands at the shoulder, but he was sleek with good clean lines. Sam checked his teeth and they showed some wear but not a lot.

"I estimate he's four or five years old. We'll get many years of service out of the animal. All right eighty-five for the horse, but only because Jo wants him so much." Sam pulled a money clip out of his pocket and peeled off one hundred and five dollars. He still had money left, too.

Jo wondered where he got his money. They didn't pay sheriffs that well in any town she'd been in before.

With a grin, Jenkins shoved the money in his pocket.

"I'll throw in a blanket for you. He grabbed a plain tan wool blanket off a stack in the stall by the saddles.

Jo's heart sang. She owned a beautiful horse and she now had a means to track down Billy Jackson. She took the bridle and walked to Smokey's stall, opened the gate and went inside, closing the gate behind her. Then she put the bridle on the animal and led him out into the stable and over to the saddles.

Sam handed her the blanket.

She tossed it on the stallion's back, followed by the saddle, moving the piece of equipment until it was fitted to the correct spot on the horse's back. Then she cinched up the straps good and tight.

"I didn't wear my riding clothes, you'll have to ride him back to the house, Sam."

"Nonsense," He patted the horse's neck. "I want to know you can handle this animal. I'm glad to see that you know how to saddle him, but I want to know that you can ride, too. So get on."

Jo looked at her husband and recognized the look of doubt on his face. He didn't think she could ride. Ha! She'd show him.

With the reins in her left hand and she grabbed the horn, put her left foot in the stirrup and pulled herself up into the saddle, swinging her right leg over the horse as she sat.

Her gingham skirt rode up, and her leg from just above the knee was exposed, along with her brown riding boots.

Mr. Jenkins' eyebrows shot up upon seeing her boots, or perhaps it was her legs that sent them skyward.

"Well, now you have a reason to wear those boots." Sam laid his hand on her thigh.

"I wrote you that I used to have a horse. I had to sell him when I came out here."

"So you did. Take Smokey here and ride home, put him in the second stall. The goats can go in with the donkey. I may get rid of the donkey now that you have this horse."

Jo frowned. "Smokey is not a pack animal."

Sam cocked his eyebrow. "If I need him to be, he is."

"Let's not fight in front of Mr. Jenkins." She tightened her grip on the reins. "We'll talk about this at home."

She turned Smokey and left the building, kicking him into a gallop as soon as she cleared the doorway, down to the main street where she slowed to a walk before turning on the street and riding out of sight.

"You've got a feisty one there, Sam." Jenkins crossed his arms over his chest as he watched Jo leave.

"I know, Paul. More independent than any woman I've ever known. I worry about her biting off more than she can chew."

"Can you handle her?"

"Oh yes, by the time I learn the truth about my wife, I'll have her eating out of my hand."

"Yes, but is that what you want, son. Based on the few times I've talked to her, she seems to be a good woman. Don't break her." He pushed his hand down slow. "Ease your way to the truth. Have you told her you're also a bounty hunter?"

Sam grinned. "No. What fun would there be in that? She has to tell me the truth first. I can't let her know that Nate told me where he'd seen her. If he hadn't been at that trial, then I might never have learned she was the one who brought Billy Jackson in."

"Did she tell you she was here asking about him yesterday?"

Sam's grin faded, and he sighed. "No. But I did get raw meat for dinner, so I think she's looking for him."

"Oh, yeah, she is." Jenkins nodded. "Are you planning on telling her I'm your pa?"

"When the time is right. I don't want to answer a lot of questions right now. Too many remain that I want answered first." Guilt knotted his gut, but he had to remember she was lying to him, too. One day they would both tell the truth and then they could move forward in their marriage.

By the time Sam got home, he saw that Jo had unsaddled Smokey and was brushing him down, talking to him as she did.

"You're such a good horse. I knew Sam would let me have you. I think he cares about me. I know I'm beginning to care for him. Maybe even love him. I know it's too soon to feel that, but I do."

She leaned against the horse with an arm over his neck. "I've never felt about anyone the way I feel about Sam. I want to please him. I feel hurt when I disappoint him like I did the other night and like I will when he finds out the truth about me. What am I going to do Smokey, when he throws me out?"

He would never throw her out. She was beginning to mean too much to him.

"Jo."

She whipped around and saw Sam settled against the frame of the door, watching her. "What are you doing here? How long have you been there?"

"First, I live here. And second, not long."

She released a pent-up breath.

"Long enough to know that you think for some reason I'll throw you out."

"Sam, I…"

He pushed off the door and walked over to her.

Sam pushed a stray strand of hair behind her ear and then cupped her jaw, raising her chin so she looked at him. "Jo, there is nothing you could tell me or you could do that would make me throw you out. You're my wife and no matter how many raw meals you make, I plan on keeping you."

Her eyes filled with tears and she sniffled, blinking quickly so as not to cry. She hated to cry, to display a weakness.

He caressed her jaw.

She leaned her head into his hand and closed her eyes.

Sam stepped closer and wrapped her in his arms.

Jo opened her eyes and looked up into the coffee-brown eyes of the man she married. The man she was quickly falling in love with.

"Sam."

"Jo."

He closed the distance between their lips taking her with such urgency he surprised her. His need for her was as great as hers for him.

"Take off your bloomers."

Pulse racing, scandalized and yet titillated by the thought of having sex outdoors, she walked to the stall they kept the hay in, removed her drawers and lay down.

Sam was there…over her…in her.

They both sighed, ready for each other. Soon after, they reached the stars, not at the same time and yet together.

He rolled off her, spent, and buttoned his pants.

At the same time she stood and then pulled on her bloomers.

"Well, that was intense." She glanced around to make sure they weren't observed and arranged her skirt. "I feel like I should be guilty for making love with my husband in the barn. Do I have any hay in my hair?" She turned her back to him.

"A little. Let me clean you up." Sam picked the pieces from her hair and kissed her on the neck. "And never feel guilty for us being together."

She shuddered need building again. She ignored the feeling.

"Let me check you." She brushed off the back of his shirt with her hands. "You're clean enough to go to work."

He turned around and clasped his arms around her waist. "I'm tempted to stay home."

"As much as I would like for you to, you can't. Dave is coming for dinner, and I have work to do. So get going."

"All right. I'm leaving." He gave her a quick kiss before walking out of the barn, headed for the jail next door.

Today was laundry day. She'd put it off last week because she didn't know how to do it. When she lived in Chicago she'd always taken her clothes to a woman who did laundry for a living. Knowing she'd have to wash the clothes someday, she'd talked to Effie and got instructions. Though the weather was a little cloudy, she thought she should be safe do get the washing finished today.

First, she filled two metal buckets with water and placed them on the stove to boil. Second, she found the large wooden tubs on the porch off the kitchen and set them upright. Third, she found the lye soap flakes and the washboard to scrub the clothes.

When the water was finally hot, she poured both buckets into the wash tub on the porch and added the soap flakes. Then she added Sam's shirts and stirred them with a large paddle.

The rinse tub held only cold water. She was assured by Effie the cold water removed the soap better.

When she thought the clothes were clean enough, she squeezed out the water by hand. The liquid was still hot and almost burned her, but she couldn't figure out any other way to do it. Then she transferred them to the rinse tub, the cold water eased the pain in her hands from the hot wash. From there she rolled the clothes into a small bundle and twisted them, wringing as much water from the garments as she could and then hung them on the line in the back yard to dry.

This process was repeated all morning and part of the afternoon until she finally had all the dirty clothes washed and hung on the clothesline.

When she was done, she took a break and ate a late lunch. Sam and Dave were eating sandwiches she'd sent with Sam that morning, after their tryst in the barn. While she ate she made notes about where she'd likely find Jackson.

Thunder roared overhead. Jo looked up and saw the dark clouds. "No! My laundry."

She ran outside. The barn door slammed open, and the donkey and goats ran out. *Damn! Didn't I latch the gate? How'd that door get open?*

The animals ran through her clean clothes, pulling them free from the clothes pins and off the line.

"Oh no." She watched as her fresh laundry fell to the muddy ground.

As she ran, she passed the donkey running the other direction wearing one of Sam's shirts on its head, the fabric caught in the animal's ears.

"Hey. Wait. Come back here with that shirt."

She saw one of the goats eating her gingham dress while another one munched on a bed sheet. Waving her arms like a wild woman, she chased away the goats.

Jo got to the basket and gathered the fallen laundry.

The donkey headed past the jail toward Main Street, still wearing Sam's shirt and the goats were missing.

She carried the laundry to the porch and dumped it in the wash tub. When she dropped the clothes into the tub, she noticed muddy goat prints headed into the kitchen.

"No." Jo ran into the living room. No goats. Checked the guest room. No goats. She closed her eyes, praying they'd gone back outside. When she went to her bedroom, she screamed. One of the goats was eating the afghan she kept at the bottom of the bed, another was in the closet munching on another one of her dresses and the last had one of Sam's good boots.

Jo pulled the boot from the goat and shooed it and its companions out of the house. She didn't care what happened to them. At this point, she was considering making them all into a stew.

She collapsed in a kitchen chair with Sam's boot on the table in front of her, a good-sized hole in the toe.

"Jo? What the hell is happening?"

She looked up and saw Sam holding his shirt.

"Disaster is happening, that's what."

"I saw the donkey run by wearing one of my shirts. Dave caught him and he's back in the barn." He laid the shirt on the table.

"I had some problems today," she admitted.

"What happened? Why is my boot on the table?"

She sighed. *Might as well tell him.* "Everything went wrong," she began and told him the whole story. She took a breath. "I hope someone eats them."

Sam looked at her. Looked at his boot, then the kitchen floor. He broke into a grin before laughing out loud.

Jo frowned. "I don't know what you think is so funny."

"Ah, Jo. I'm sorry." His eyes sparkled with merriment. "I've wanted to laugh since I saw the donkey, but I'm now imagining the goats in here and can't help myself."

"Take a look at your boot." She picked it off the table and shook it. "You'll stop laughing."

"No, I won't. They were only boots. The main thing is you're all right. You didn't get injured in all the mayhem."

"No, but I have to redo all the laundry." She remembered the muddy lump and shuddered.

"Not today you don't. It's still raining. Might as well leave it all until tomorrow.

Come on now. Admit it, now that it's over. Seeing the donkey with the shirt on was funny."

She sniffed, then smiled and then laughed. "Yes, it was. That poor animal." Leaning forward she clutched her sides. "And then the goats, eating the bed and your boots. Oh, my gosh."

Sam's laughter subsided somewhat. "You can try again tomorrow. "

She nodded. "Tomorrow."

*****

Billy Jackson hadn't seen her yet, but he knew she was here in Hope's Crossing. The bitch who caught him and would have had him hanged if not for Frank Bauer. Frank's gang broke him out on the way to Joliet and Billy was a lucky beneficiary of that breakout. Then Frank decided to go with Billy and head west. He'd heard stories of the gold in the Montana Territory, there just for the taking.

Billy didn't care about the gold, all he wanted was her. Jo Shafter. He wanted her to pay. Like her family had paid. Rex Shafter should never have come after Billy, regardless of the size of the bounty on his head. If he hadn't Rex and his family might still be alive, but he had come after him and then his daughter had done the same. So, she had to die. It was that simple. Cross Billy Jackson and give up your life.

He knew where she was, and that was the problem. She'd married Sam Longworth, sheriff of Hope's Crossing in the Montana Territory. Billy knew him by reputation. He was a well-known bounty hunter. Sam worked everything west of the Mississippi, but mostly the Colorado, Wyoming and Montana Territories. Jo had worked in Illinois and Missouri. Billy thought it ironic that the two of them had probably never met before as bounty hunters and yet ended up married.

Billy knew Sam because Billy had plied his trade in the Colorado Territory, in Central City and their paths had crossed. Could he possibly be lucky enough to remove two of the thorns in his side at once?

CHAPTER 6

A week after the laundry fiasco, Jo decided to try her hand at making bread. She had been buying bread, baked by one of the local women, from the mercantile, but the loaf was never hot and she wanted to prove to Sam that she could make anything, if she had a recipe.

She'd bought the yeast at the mercantile and had all the other ingredients already. Jo mixed the flour and the rest of the dry ingredients together and kneaded it into a ball, then she greased a large mixing bowl and dropped the dough inside to rise. The cookbook said it should be put in a warm place but could be left overnight, if necessary. She put the bowl on the counter in the sunshine but was sure the bread would be fine while she was out hunting for Jackson.

Jo donned her denim's, flannel shirt and her gun then she went out to the barn and saddled Smokey. She walked him out of the barn, closed the barn doors tight and mounted and rode in the opposite direction of the jail.

She'd lost Jackson's tracks at the edge of town yesterday, so she'd try to pick them up again today. Since there hadn't been any rain or snow, finding and following the tracks should be easy enough.

Jo rode around the edge of town. She didn't want Sam, or anyone else, to see her dressed the way she was. Not with her gun on and wearing denims and a shirt. She'd almost put on her buckskins but it was an especially warm day for early May.

Upon reaching the same spot where she'd lost his tracks a few days ago, she dismounted and walked in a wide circle looking for where they picked up again. Finally she found the hoof-prints and the pine branch used to sweep the area clear. Jackson was smart, she'd give him that, but she was smarter.

For several hours, she followed the tracks. They were steadily headed away from town, which was what she expected. Suddenly, the markings took a sharp turn and started back the way she'd come. He was headed back to town. Why come out here all this way and then circle back?

A frisson of fear went up her spine. Was she in a trap? Jo drew her gun and looked around but she didn't see anything or anyone.

Jackson was getting to her and she'd had enough for today. She kicked Smokey into a gallop back toward town. She'd only gone about five miles west of town, so the trip back wouldn't take long. She'd have plenty of time to clean up and bake her bread before Sam came home.

Jo arrived back at the barn and unsaddled Smokey, curried him, and then brushed him. He'd proved to be as deep-chested as she thought and he was fast. She'd galloped almost the whole way back to town and he didn't even seem winded. After she finished his grooming she gave him a bucket of oats, fresh water and a flake of hay. He'd earned it.

Jo went inside and took off her denims, washed herself clean of the smell of horse and donned her pink calico dress. Then she walked into the kitchen to finish the bread in time for dinner.

When she saw what awaited her on the counter, she screamed, "No. This can't be happening."

The bread had risen out of the bowl, over the sides and on to the counter. She lit the stove, added wood, and started the oven heating. She would make this mess into bread if it killed her.

She pulled the sticky mixture off the counter, deposited it back in the bowl and punched the dough down as best she could. Then she floured the counter and poured the dough onto it, where she pushed and pulled the dough into the shape of loaves. The bread would be very light, but hopefully the taste would still be good.

She glanced down at the pin watch on her dress and saw she only had about an hour and a half until Sam arrived home wanting dinner. She took the loaves she'd formed and situated them on a cookie sheet before placing her hand in the oven to check the temperature. When she could only keep her hand in the oven about five seconds, the temperature was correct and she put the bread inside. The recipe said the baking time was thirty to forty-five minutes depending on the oven. She'd check the bread at fifteen minutes, to see how it was doing, turn it and continue to rotate it every fifteen minutes to make sure that no one area was against the fire side of the oven for the entire cooking time. Very easy to burn it on one side and have it raw on the other, as she could attest from her first efforts using this oven.

For the rest of the meal, she had pork chops to fry and potatoes to boil. She prepared the food and started it all cooking. Then she sat and looked at her list of all the places that Jackson could hide. The list showed plenty of places that, because she was a woman, she couldn't go. Saloons and whorehouses mostly and Hope's Crossing had plenty of both. In Illinois she had a man, Jessup, she'd used for those places. He would go in and if the target was inside, he'd chase him out where Jo could get him.

Now she didn't have that luxury. If she wasn't married to Sam and wouldn't embarrass him to death, she'd go into the places herself to check them out. For this capture, she needed to decide what was more important—keeping her secret or getting her quarry.

According to her pin watch it was time to check the bread. Jo opened the oven and saw…a mess. She closed her eyes hoping she was having a bad dream and would wake. No such luck. The loaves had spread so she had one large, cookie sheet sized loaf of bread rather than the three she started with. She checked the recipe to see if she used too much yeast but she'd used the right amount. The recipe must have been printed wrong. Jo wanted to cry but refused.

The bread looked tasty even if it wasn't the right shape. The loaf was golden brown on one side and smelled wonderful. She turned the pan so the opposite side was next to the fire box. After the loaf had baked for forty five minutes and was golden brown all over, she removed it from the oven. She let the giant loaf, which resembled corn bread, cool while she put the fried pork chops in a baking pan and slid them in the oven to finish cooking. Then she mashed the potatoes and made cream gravy with the drippings from the chops.

"I'm home. Is dinner ready?" Sam's deep baritone brought her back to reality and away from thinking about Billy Jackson.

"It's ready, but you might not want to eat the bread."

"At least nothing looks raw."

She planted her hands on her hips. "You won't let me forget that, will you?"

"Nope." He grinned.

Jo lifted her cheek for him to buss. She started the habit to get a kiss on the cheek when he came home, but he always grabbed her up for a real, full-blown kiss. Sam was a passionate man and he liked to kiss. At least he liked to kiss her.

"What do you see on the counter next to the sink?" She jutted her chin in that direction.

"What?" He stopped and looked over toward the sink. "What's on the cookie sheet? That doesn't look like cookies."

"It's bread. Before I...uh...noticed, the dough had risen out of the bowl and all over the counter. I'm lucky it didn't hit the floor. Anyway, I don't have any bread pans, so the loaves I made just flowed together and made one big flat loaf."

He came behind her and laid his hands

on her shoulders. "I'm sure it tastes fine and that's all that matters, not how it looks."

"Well, why don't you cut a piece and see?"

"All right I will."

He took a knife out of the drawer, cut a square off the bread and tasted it.

"It's good. Where's the butter?"

She pointed toward the icebox. "In the crock."

He used the same knife and buttered the tasty morsel in his hand. After he finished that piece, he cut himself another.

"Well?"

"Can't you tell? I'm on my second piece. Do you really think I would have gone to a second one if it was terrible?"

"You could just be being kind."

"Trust me. I like this. It may not look like regular bread, but it sure as heck tastes like it. I'd say you did pretty well. Why don't you pick up some loaf pans at the mercantile next time you go?"

"I will." Jo smiled, happy that the situation had turned out fine after all.

*****

He watched her come out of the forest exactly where he had and then she lost his trail in the midst of all the other tracks entering and leaving town, just as he wanted her to. Now she knew for sure he was here, in town. He wanted her to find him. That was part of the game. She would take time to find him but that was time he would use to prepare for her. He didn't want to give himself away too soon. He had some surprises for Jo Shafter…no, that wasn't right. Her name was Jo Longworth now.

He wanted to take her down. Wanted her to suffer like her father had. He wanted her to watch while he killed Sam Longworth. But he needed Jo to bring in Sam. One couldn't happen without the other.

*****

The next day, Jo made lunch for Sam and Dave and took it to them. Sam had tried to tell her that she was expected to bring him lunch every day. She told him that she had work to do and he could come home or she would prepare lunch in the morning for him to take.

When she walked in Jo saw Sam talking to a man who was not very happy. She recognized the portly man with the balding head as Mayor John Greenbush. The mayor was wearing the same brown suit and vest with a white shirt that he always wore.

"Sam what will you do about my roses?" The mayor was red faced and shaking his fist at Sam. "My mother planted those bushes, and your goats have eaten them nearly to the ground?"

"Sam. Mayor Greenbush." Jo carried the basket to Dave's desk and set it down. "Am I to understand that the goats I inadvertently let loose have wreaked havoc in your yard?"

"Um, yes, Mrs. Longworth." The mayor glanced at his raised fist and quickly put it behind his back. "They have, and I was just asking the sheriff what reparations he'll make."

"Sam didn't have anything to do with the goats getting loose, and I don't believe he should be held accountable for the damage." Jo went around the desk and put her hand on Sam's shoulder. "I'm the one who is responsible for your roses being eaten. Please, let me make it right."

"How do you propose to do that?"

"Sam has a rose bush in his front yard. Let me see if I can get a clipping to grow, and once it does, I'll plant it in your yard to replace your mother's roses. If it doesn't grow, I'll replant Sam's entire rose bush in your yard. I know it's not the same, but it's the best I can do."

The mayor mopped the sweat from his brow, his gaze flipping from Sam to Jo. "Well, I don't know."

Jo thought the mayor looked like he really wanted to have Sam pay him for the roses but when Jo offered to replace them he couldn't very well say no, now could he.

"I guess that will have to do. Thank you, Mrs. Longworth."

"No, it is I who should thank you, and apologize for the damage the goats caused. I'll do my best to round them up. Can you tell me where you saw them last?"

"They were running from me and my shotgun. Headed east, out of town. If they know what's good for them, they'll keep running."

Jo's hand flew to her mouth and she lowered her head to keep from laughing.

"So John, are we good here?" Sam came around to the front of his desk.

"Yes. We're fine." He turned to Jo. "I'll expect to see that new rose bush planted this year."

"You will, Mr. Mayor. I promise."

The man nodded, turned and left.

After she saw he was out of the office, Jo burst into laughter.

"I don't know what you're laughing at." Sam tried to keep a stern face, but when he looked at Jo, he started to smile and then he was laughing, too.

"Do you think the goats have stopped running yet?"

Sam shook his head. "I wouldn't have if I were them. But we do need to get them back. The nannies will need milking and the mercantile wants their supply."

Jo stood with her hands clasped in front of her. "Yes, I suppose we should try to round them up."

"Paul's stable is on the east end of town, why don't we start there and work our way back. You up for a walk?"

She shook her head and pointed at the basket on Dave's desk. "You have to eat your lunch first. Where is Dave? I brought food for him, too."

"What did you make for us today?"

"Leftovers from that roast we had two nights ago. That flat bread worked very well for the sandwiches. Plus I made potato salad and a couple of pieces of pie were left."

Sam walked over to her, gathered her in

his arms, and gave her a kiss.

"I'd rather have you for lunch."

He gave her another kiss.

This one didn't hold back any of his passion.

She broke the kiss and pushed at his chest. "Sam, we can't."

He sighed. "A man can dream can't he?"

"Behave and eat your lunch and then tonight we'll go look for the goats.

"Yes, ma'am."

He moved aside the paper on his desk.

She opened the basket and removed the dishes.

Jo settled in the chair at the side of Sam's desk and ate one of the six sandwiches she'd made.

"This potato salad is really good."

Sam licked his lips.

"I think you're cooking's getting better and better."

"Thank you. I appreciate that you've noticed."

"Oh, I've noticed. I haven't had a raw piece of meat since that first time I brought Dave home for dinner."

The door opened. "Did I hear my name being taken in vain?"

Dave walked across the floor leading a goat tied to the end of a piece of rope.

Jo jumped up. "You found one of our goats."

"Yes, ma'am and I'm putting him into a jail cell until we find the other two."

"That's a great idea. Thanks, Dave," said Sam.

Dave used the big key ring to unlock one of the two jail cells and led the goat inside, took off the rope and hurried out before the goat could follow, slamming the door shut behind him.

"That ought to keep him out of trouble."

"I don't know about that." Jo pointed at the cell where the goat was happily eating the wool blanket on the cot.

"Hey!"

Dave opened the cell.

Scampering and sliding, the goat tried to run past him.

"Oh, no you don't." He quickly shut the cell door. "Give me that." Dave pulled the blanket from the goat who didn't seem to mind. He simply started chewing on the cot's mattress.

"No, you don't get to eat that either. Sam," Dave raised his voice. "Come get your goat before we don't have anything left in this cell."

Sam and Jo were both laughing.

Jo tried to stop but as soon as she did, the goat took another bite of the mattress and she got the giggles again.

Sam took the piece of rope that Dave had used to get the goat there and went into the cell with it.

Jo watched the goat wait until Sam and Dave were tangled up with each other in the tiny cell, then he shot through the open door into the main office.

"Come here, Jasper." Jo patted her leg.

The goat trotted over like a well-behaved dog.

Muttering, Sam came out of the cell and handed her the rope.

With an easy move, she tied the cord around the goat's neck and kept the other end in hand so he wouldn't run again.

"If you can get him to come to you, why didn't you do it before, when they were in the house?" asked Sam.

"The nannies don't listen to me, and he was following them. Now if we find the other two down by Paul's stable, we can relax and so can the mayor.

Twenty minutes later they got very lucky. Paul *had* caught the other two miscreant goats much to his dismay. They were eating the wool blankets he kept in the barn stall to sell along with the saddles. He trapped them in the stall with the blankets and gave them a flake of hay to eat, hoping they'd leave his horse blankets alone.

Paul and Sam tied rope around each goat's neck so Jo and Sam could walk them home. Once there, Sam put them back in the stall and closed the gate securely.

By the time they got into the house it was already three o'clock.

"I don't want to go back and sit for two hours. I'm going to tell Dave I won't be back tonight."

He walked next door.

As soon as he left, Jo looked toward the ceiling. "Dang it. No tracking Billy today."

When he returned, Jo asked, "What would you like to eat tonight.

Sam looked back at her and she recognized that expression. He wanted to spend the afternoon in bed.

"You can just get that look out of your eyes. I'm not making love to you this afternoon. I have too much to do before supper."

He wrapped his arms around her waist. "Oh? And what is it that you have to do that can't be put off?"

Jo thought fast, "I have to go shopping. I need something to cook for dinner and I thought I'd check out some of the other stores."

"Everything you need is as the mercantile."

"I just thought I'd check out the rest of the town, on my own. I don't want to take you away from your duties."

"That's nice but it's not a problem. I'll take you around—"

"No." She lifted her hands and laid them on his chest. "Really I want to do it by myself. I need to look around and meet people on my own."

"All right." Sam shook his head and shrugged. "Fine. I'll see you for dinner."

"See you then." She leaned forward, cheek first, for a kiss.

Like he always did, Sam turned her head and gave her a real kiss on the lips that left her breathless.

"How do you do that? Every time you kiss me my heart pounds and I become short of breath."

"You must be in love with me." Sam cocked an eyebrow.

She shook her head. "Don't be ridiculous. We don't know each other well enough to be in love."

"I said you were in love. Not me. I don't have any intention of falling head over heels for you."

Her breath caught in her throat. "So you're saying you'll never love me?"

He shrugged. "I'm simply stating facts. I won't fall for you or for any woman. I did once and I don't intend to do so again."

"She must have hurt you badly."

"She did." He turned away from her. "She died."

Jo's hand flew to her mouth. "I'm so sorry. I didn't know."

He looked out the window above the sink. "My wife died in a stage coach accident. She was leaving me. Didn't like the life I led. She said I was gone too much and she wanted to go to New York anyway. My wife hated it here. Too primitive for her. Do you feel that way, Jo? Is this way of life and living in this town too hard for you?"

She lay her hand on his arm. "No, Sam. I

like it here and I like you."

He grinned. "I'm glad to hear you like it here…and you love me."

"I don't." She thought back to the day she'd spoken all her secrets to Smokey. "You can say something as often as you like, but that doesn't make it true."

He cocked his head to one side. "We'll see."

CHAPTER 7

The valley they lived in was one of the prettiest places Jo had ever been. They were surrounded by the lower foothills, covered in trees, green grasses and wild explosions of color from all the different kinds of wild flowers. These hills gave way to tall mountains, whose peaks were covered in snow year round. These were the Rocky Mountains, glorious, magical places.

Hope's Crossing had everything one could want, which made the reason Sam's wife left him that much more unbelievable. Sure, maybe Hope's Crossing wasn't as settled as Denver and it didn't have the large stores or selection of merchandise as New York or Chicago, but the folks at the mercantile could order anything a body could need or want.

In her mind she heard Sam's voice when she arrived, telling her as if by rote. "Two miles south of town was Nevada City, an even smaller mining settlement. Together the two settlements have about 1200 residents, most of which were single men. Of the nineteen women living in the two settlements, twelve of them are prostitutes, all living here in Hope's Crossing."

Not that Jo cared, everyone needed to make a living one way or another and if those women chose that way of life...well, that was their choice. Most women wouldn't want to do what Jo did either. Bounty hunting took a special kind of temperament and stamina. It wasn't an easy way to earn money but it was rewarding. Taking the scum out of circulation and putting them in prison was very satisfying. It was something she had to admit she missed. Being a wife wasn't exactly exciting, but then there was Sam. She cared very much for Sam, more than she ever thought she would.

If only she could tell Sam. Maybe he'd

understand. Maybe he was telling her the truth and he wouldn't throw her out. Could she risk it? If she couldn't find Billy herself she would have no choice.

Jo put on her buckskins as soon as Sam left for his office. She was buckling the gun around her waist when she heard the unmistakable sound of boots coming to a stop behind her. Turning, gun drawn, she looked her husband in the eyes.

She took a deep breath and holstered her weapon. "That's a good way to get killed, coming upon a person unannounced." She finished tying the leather laces that held the holster in place, around her thigh.

"Where do you think you're going dressed like that?"

His voice held no anger, only curiosity.

She swallowed hard. "After a man named Billy Jackson."

"We need to talk, Jo."

Sam came up behind her and placed his hands on her shoulders and gave her a little squeeze.

"It's past time we got everything out in the open. Come to the front room."

Jo followed while donning her soft leather buckskin coat.

Sam sank into one of the big chairs by the fireplace.

On a normal day, Jo would have seated herself on the settee next to his chair, but this wasn't a normal day. Today, she was ending her marriage by the looks of it. Instead she sat in the chair at the other end of the sofa and crossed her legs.

Sam waved his hand up and down. "Why are you wearing those clothes?"

Jo took a deep breath, uncrossed her legs and leaned forward, arms on her knees. "I'm a bounty hunter. I thought I could let all of that be in my past and be the kind of wife you want, but I can't." She sat upright and looked at Sam, making sure her gaze was unwavering. "Not yet. The man who murdered my family escaped from jail and is here. Until I learn he's either behind bars again or dead, I'm hunting him."

"I wondered when you would tell me." He let out a breath and folded his hands in front of him. "I know Jackson escaped and I know you were a bounty hunter. Nate told me. He was at Jackson's trial. The trial judge is a friend of his."

Jo muttered an expletive under her breath. "I'd hoped I was wrong and he didn't recognize me when we got married. How long have you known?"

"Since the day after our wedding. Nate came to the office to tell me."

She stood and went to the fireplace, putting both hands on the mantle and leaning her body onto her arms. "So what happens now?" She swallowed hard, the words hard to get by the lump in her throat. She turned around. "Will you divorce me?"

"No, but I am forbidding you to go after this man." He looked her up and down. "And to wear those clothes again."

She shook her head. "You might as well divorce me. I'm not stopping until I have Jackson. He's here. In Hope's Crossing or close by. I've just got to find him."

"I'll find him."

She stared at him her hands in fists. "You don't know what he looks like. I do. It was my family he murdered not yours. And if that isn't clear enough, then I'll say it plainly." She leaned over and jabbed him in the chest with her index finger. "Over my dead body."

Narrowing his gaze, he captured her hand with his. "You're my wife. I can't allow you take chances like that anymore.

And I do know what you're feeling. Rex Shafter was a friend of mine."

Gasping, she leaned back and blinked several times. "You knew my father?"

Sam got up and paced in front of the cold fireplace.

"As long as things are coming out into the open, you should know about me, too. I was a bounty hunter for a few of my thirty years, and I ran into your father periodically. Usually when we were after the same man." A half-smile turned up the corners of his mouth. "Your father usually beat me to those bounties. He was the best tracker I ever knew." He stopped his pacing in front of her. "What I didn't know is that he had a beautiful daughter."

Jo put her hands in her pockets and looked at the floor hoping he didn't see her blush.

"But a useless daughter when it comes to the feminine arts." She looked up into his face. "I was raised as Rex's son for the first twenty years of my life and spent the last five tracking Billy Jackson and his gang. I learned very little in all my twenty-five years about how to cook and sew and keep a house. I'm learning all that now as I go."

Sam chuckled. "That was fairly obvious the night of the raw roast for dinner."

She smiled with him. Now the incident was funny, but it hadn't been at the time. Then her smile turned to a frown. "Why didn't I know you? I rode with Papa lots of times, and I don't remember you. I would definitely have remembered someone who looked like you."

Sam cocked his eyebrow, moved forward and wrapped her in his arms. "I'm glad you find me pleasing."

Unwilling to fall under his spell, she pushed out of his embrace. "Don't get off the subject. What do you plan on doing, now that you know who and what I am?"

He ran his hand around the back of his neck. "Nothing to do. We're married and I decide how you will act." Sam returned his gaze to her. "There will be no divorce and no more bounty hunting for you."

Jo shook her head and backed up a couple of steps. Her father had never treated her mother in such a way. "How dare you treat me like a piece of chattel. I'll file the divorce papers myself then, because I'm not stopping until Billy Jackson is back in custody or dead. I prefer dead myself, but

I'll take either."

Sam closed the distance between them and grabbed her by the upper arms. "You will not divorce me. Do you understand? No divorce." He kissed her hard. He almost punished her with his lips.

She broke away and wiped her mouth with the back of her hand. "Then we are at an impasse, because I won't stop looking for Jackson. He's here in town and I'll find him. Right now he's toying with me. He knows who I am and where to find me but for some reason he hasn't come forward."

"Of course." He threw out his arm. "He's trying to set you up. He wants you to lose everything like he did when you sent him to jail."

She remembered her family. Her father with his booming laugh. Her mother, fussing about Jo's dress the first time she wore one as an adult. And Robby, fishing beside her down at the local creek. "He already took everything from me and he knows it."

"You weren't married then. Now he wants to take me from you, too."

Jo hadn't wanted to give a voice to that particular idea. That would acknowledge that Sam meant something to her. Jackson couldn't know that. Heck, Jo was just now realizing that Sam was very important.

"We've only been married a few weeks. Why would I mourn your loss?"

Sam moved forward and rubbed her arms up and down, slowly, gently. "Wouldn't you? Mourn my loss?"

Unable to answer the question she saw in his eyes, Jo looked away. "Maybe."

She thought she was in love with her husband. How silly was that? She'd only known him for a few weeks, but the feelings were there, easy enough to see for anyone who really looked...like Sam was looking now.

He took her chin with this thumb and forefinger and turned her head toward him.

"Look at me, Jo."

"No." She looked at the floor, her boots, anywhere but at him.

"Please. Jo."

She raised her gaze to his beautiful coffee brown eyes.

"I care for you, too."

He lowered his head, his lips taking hers gently.

She wrapped her arms around his neck and greedily savaged his lips. Jo didn't want gentle. She wanted hard and fierce. She wanted Sam to make her forget everything except him.

He jerked her hard against him and ravaged her mouth before pulling back.

Sam rested his head against hers while he held her close and whispered in her ear.

"What am I to do with you?"

"Let me go," she whispered and pulled back, out of his arms, putting distance between them. "Let me find him. Let me finish this."

"No. I can't let you go…by yourself. I'll go along."

That was an answer she hadn't been prepared for.

"Co…come with me? But what about your job? You have people to protect and fights to break up and whatever other tasks you do. You can't come with me."

"Jo, I was once a bounty hunter, just like you." He ran his hand behind his neck. "I worked with your father on several occasions. I was shocked and saddened by his murder and rejoiced when his killer was caught. I just didn't know that Jo Shafter was a woman, not a man."

She shook her head. "You can't, you

took an oath to protect the people of this town."

"Finding and arresting Jackson, is part of my job and *is* protecting the people of this town."

She narrowed her eyes. "Jackson is mine. At this point, I don't care about the bounty. I only care that I take him into custody and that he knows it's me who's bringing him in. Again. I want him to know I'm smarter than he is, and that he can't get away from me. If he hadn't followed me here, then as soon as I heard he escaped, I would have left to track him down. Are you sure you want to be married to me knowing that?"

He walked to stand in front of her and placed his hands on her shoulders. "I'm sure. I care for you. I may not fall in love with you, but I will admit that I care for you and don't want to see you killed."

Jo was saddened and yet encouraged, by his words. He would try hard not to fall in love with her, yet she thought caring was a good first step.

She stood with her fists at her sides. "I won't be killed. I'm faster than Jackson."

Sam looked toward the heavens and

shook his head. "You really think he'll fight you in a fair gunfight? He'll ambush you and then he'll kill you after he's made you suffer. He's a killer and the sooner you realize that the better."

"I know that. I brought him in the first time. Remember?"

"I remember. I also think Jackson has gotten smarter since then."

"So have I."

Sam rubbed his hands over his face.

She could tell he was giving in.

She waited.

Finally, he nodded. "So where did you lose his tracks?"

He sounded resigned to the fact that she would not let this go.

She would never let Jackson go. He would pay for killing her family, even if the only way was for her to kill him herself.

"About five miles west of here, he turned and headed back to town. The hour was late and I had to get home, so I don't know where he actually reentered, or where he went after that. I don't know that I could have picked up his trail once he hit town anyway. Too many other hoof prints with people coming and going to Nevada City, or the mines farther up the canyon."

Sam scratched his jaw. "There're several whorehouses and saloons down that way. He could be in anyone of them and likely the owner wouldn't tell us if he was."

"We need someone who isn't known to them to go inside and ask. Someone who would pass as a dangerous drifter. Know anyone like that?"

"I might. It's a known bounty hunter strategy, after all."

He paused.

It was as if he contemplating something very serious.

He looked her in the eyes. "As long as we're sharing our secrets, I should tell you that Paul Jenkins is my father. In his younger days he was a bank robber. He gave all that up when he met and married my mother. He never murdered anyone and the statute of limitations have long run out on his crimes, but if he shaved his beard, no one in town would know him. He could be our man on the inside and let us know which establishment Jackson is in."

Jo's mouth dropped open and she had to blink several times to get her mind to focus.

"Paul is your father?"

"Yes, and he was a bank robber."

She didn't say anything. She couldn't. What if she said the wrong thing? Paul was Sam's father. Well, what else would Sam spring on her today?

CHAPTER 8

"Jo. Talk to me."

She took a deep breath. "How could you keep something like that from me?"

"I wasn't ready for you to know. Paul has worked hard to put that part of his life behind him. He was…is…a good father. We both decided the circumstance would be best if people didn't know he was my father."

"But why? If he's no longer wanted for the robberies and he's been an upstanding citizen, why would you keep it a secret? And why is your name Longworth not Jenkins?"

"Playing it safe. I wanted to be a lawman. Bounty hunting was just a way to earn money and I was good at it. As to my name, we thought Longworth, my mother's maiden name, was a safer choice. Dad became Paul Jenkins when he married my mother."

She narrowed her gaze. "You never answered my question. Why haven't I heard of you, especially if you rode with my dad?"

He placed both hands on the mantle and looked into the hearth, his back to her.

"I was called the man from Montana in those days or just Montana."

She couldn't believe it. After all these years and all her father's stories, she was finally meeting Montana. And she was married to him! "You're Montana? Dad talked about you." She smiled. "He said you were *almost* as good as he was."

"That's probably true. Everyone knew your dad was the best."

"I learned everything from him. I'm the best I know and I'll get Jackson...before you do."

He turned from the fireplace and looked at her. "Want to bet?"

She squared her shoulders and jutted out her chin. "What will you give me if I win?"

"What do you want?"

"I want you to hire a cook to teach me how, and then to stay on and work for us. We'll need the help when we have children, anyway."

"You'll have her. Even if I have to go to Denver or San Francisco to find her."

"And if I lose?" asked Jo, butterflies in her stomach.

"I get breakfast in bed for a week, served by you, naked as the day you were born."

She grinned. "I'd say either way is a win for me."

He lifted an eyebrow. "I'm very glad you think so."

"Shall we leave? I'm ready to find one Billy Jackson, wanted…dead or alive."

"First we talk to Paul."

She followed him out of the house and they saddled their horses. The hour was late and they'd be out tonight, so while Sam tied on their bedrolls, Jo prepared food to take with them. Regardless of what Paul said, they were tracking Jackson and would find where he was holed up.

"Whoa," said Jo to Smokey when they got to the stable. She slipped her boots out of the stirrups and dismounted.

Sam was beside her as they walked inside.

"Paul." Sam called out.

Jenkins came out of one of the stalls with a pitchfork in his hand.

"Sam. Jo. What can I do for you? Surely you're not here to buy another horse so soon. What you dressed up like that for, Jo?"

"Never mind Jo," said Sam. "We have a proposition to discuss with you."

Paul leaned on the pitchfork.

"I'm listening."

"First…" Jo looked over at Paul. "Sam told me all about you. I'm glad you reformed but now we need you to be the person you were before. You need to be a little dangerous and go places that Sam and I can't. Sam because he's the sheriff and me because I'm a woman."

Paul narrowed his eyes and shifted his gaze between the two. "What kind of places are you talking about?"

"Places that Billy Jackson might hang out," said Sam.

Jo hooked her thumbs in her pockets. "Saloons and whorehouses, for the most part," explained Jo.

"They would know me in some of those

places." Paul set the pitchfork against the first stall door. "I've been known to partake of a drink now and again."

"You'd have to shave your beard," Jo waved her hand up and down in front of him. "You'd have to wear different clothes. We can probably find what you need at the mercantile."

"No need. I can provide my own clothes and my own weapon, too. Just because I went straight doesn't mean I didn't prepare for the worst and hope for the best." He squared his shoulders. "I have my things from that time of my life."

Sam raised an eyebrow. "Will you still fit them? You're not exactly a young buck anymore."

"Don't you be sassin' me, boy. I still wear the same size I always did."

Sam smiled. "Whatever you say, old man."

Jo was surprised at the playfulness of the two men. Their attitude was so different than when she was here before. Now that she knew their secret, they could be themselves and didn't have to play the part of strangers.

"I don't think I'd recognize you without that beard," said Sam. "You've had it for as long as I can remember."

"I didn't have it when I met your mother."

Jo saw a gentle countenance come over Paul.

"When Martha and I married and I decided to go straight, I grew the beard. I wanted to keep your mother safe and then when you came along, I needed to protect you, too."

Sam put his hand on the older man's shoulder. "You did fine, Dad. Just fine. Mom and I were safe and, until you told me when I was fifteen, I never would have believed you were Virgil James."

Jo's eyes widened. "You're Virgil James? I heard stories about you when I was growing up. You're the only one of the Colton gang they never caught."

"I am." Paul's face clouded over. "I'm not proud of those years of my life. As far as I'm concerned, my life started when I met and married Martha."

"She must have been a special woman," said Jo.

"Yes, she was." He gave a quick nod. "She gave me Sam and an existence I never thought possible. She made me want to be a different man. For her. For my boy."

"So, will you do it?" asked Sam.

He seemed agitated at the road the conversation took. Like he didn't want to discuss his mother. Jo would let it go for now, but sometime soon he needed to tell her what happened to Martha.

"I will," said Paul. "If I can help take a murderer off the street then I'll do it. I never killed anyone in all the years I was with the gang. I don't cotton to varmints that take someone else's life."

Paul looked over at Jo.

"Sam told me what happened to your family. I'm sorry for your loss and I understand your need to see the man responsible brought to justice. I don't know that I could have taken him in like you did. Instead, I probably would have killed him. You've got a lot of grit, girl. I like that."

Jo felt the heat come to a point in her cheeks. "Thanks. I wanted to, believe me. I wanted him to give me an excuse, any excuse but he didn't. Now though…now is different. I feel it. This time the situation will come down to him or me and I intend to win that showdown."

Sam put his arm around her shoulder.

"We'll find him and put him behind bars…together."

*****

Billy Jackson lay in bed, an arm crooked behind his head.

The redhead there with him, slept soundly, little snorts coming from her open mouth.

He'd worn her out, but he'd paid for the whole night and didn't care. She was just a whore and he'd needed a woman.

He could think, now that his body had a release. Jo must be getting very frustrated at not finding him, but that's what he wanted. He wanted her to get too anxious and make a mistake.

He'd sold the horse he bought at the stable to a man who was headed to the gold fields, then bought himself another from a miner who was giving up and returning home to Pennsylvania. As a disguise, he'd shaved his beard and only had a mustache now.

Billy needed to see what Jo was up to, discreetly, of course. He woke the sleeping woman next to him.

"Get up and get out."

She turned over, her naked breast

teasing him to continue their activities from the night before. But, he had things to do that didn't include another interlude with the red-head. At least, not this morning.

"Will I see you tonight, honey?" She pushed the thick mass of red hair out of her eyes.

"Probably. We'll have to see how my day goes. Now git."

She scrambled out of bed, threw a flimsy chemise over her head and hooked her corset up the front, to just under her breasts. Then she tied her skirt around her waist and put on her shoes.

"See you later, honey." She turned and left the room.

Good. Now he could think. He'd go down to the hotel and get a room. The old lady who ran the place would surely tell Jo, she had a red-haired customer. Then what? He could wait for her to come to him or better yet, lead her on a merry chase through the countryside. She'd caught him last time because he'd remained too long in one place. He wouldn't make that mistake again. No, this time he'd make when she found him and he'd be ready.

She wouldn't take him by surprise.

Though, he had a little surprise for her. He walked to the room next to his and opened the door without knocking.

"Finish up and get ready. We're leaving," he said to the man in the bed pumping hard into a blonde.

At Billy's words, he pumped harder and shouted his release. Then he rolled off her.

"Get out," Frank said, his voice more gravely than usual.

The woman gathered her things and quickly left the room.

Billy figured she was probably ready to go if the split lip she bore was any indication. He liked rough sex, but never saw the point in hurting the girl. Billy wanted her with as much vigor as possible so she could keep up with his activities. Beating her would serve no purpose.

"What do you want?" Frank leaned back on the headboard and lit a cheroot and took a drink from the bottle of whiskey next to the bed.

"I want you sober."

Billy took the whiskey from the brown-haired man and sat on the end of the bed.

Frank needed a shave. Several days of dark stubble shadowed his face and a bath wouldn't do either one of them any harm. Besides, the hot water would get Frank sober quicker.

"When are you finishing with the bounty hunter? We need to get to the gold fields before it's all gone."

"Soon. You'll be able to go soon, but I need you now. She'll be surprised to find that I have an accomplice and I need that advantage."

"What if that sheriff she married shows up with her? According to Flossie, he's got a reputation for being fast."

"He can be as fast as he wants. I don't intend to give him a chance to be fast or slow."

Frank leered. "Gonna shoot him in the back, huh?"

"If I have to I will. If he's smart, he'll stay out of this difficulty between Jo and me."

"Difficulty? Difficulty?" Frank rolled over on the bed, laughing. "You do have a way with words, Jackson."

Billy Jackson's lips turned up at the corners but according to the redhead the amusement never reached his eyes. Eyes so dark a brown they looked black. The redhead called them dead eyes.

*****

Paul disappeared inside the tack room and changed his clothes. He came back wearing black wool pants, a black shirt and leather vest. Two pearl-handled revolvers were on his belt, the holsters a few inches below the hem of the vest.

"Well?" he asked as he walked from back of the stable. "What do you think? Will I do?"

Jo's eyes widened as Paul came closer. He looked dangerous, and even though she knew he wasn't, she involuntarily reached for her gun. A moment passed.

Relaxing, she moved her hand back to the waist of her pants where she hooked her thumbs. "I'd say you'll do. And without your beard…I could pass you on the street and wouldn't know you."

"She's right, Dad. You look like a totally different person."

"Thanks, I think." Paul tugged on his vest and set it straight.

Sam looked at his father from head to toe. "Something's missing." Then he snapped his fingers. "A hat. Preferably a Stetson with a wide brim."

Jo furrowed her brows. "Why a wide brim?"

"So he can wear it down to cover his eyes. He'll look more dangerous that way." Sam showed her with his own hat.

Paul walked back to the tack room and returned a short time later.

"You mean like this one?"

He wore a dusty black Stetson with a flat top and wide brim.

"Yes," said Sam. "That's perfect. So different from the flannel shirt and leather apron you usually wear."

"You look like the Virgil James of legend," said Jo, aware of the touch of awe in her voice.

"When this is over, these clothes will go back in storage. Just a memory of another life," said Paul. "As an outlaw, I probably wouldn't have survived long enough to have seen my son come into the world, much less watch him grow up. I wouldn't have had more than twenty years with my beautiful Martha, the only woman I'll ever love, if I hadn't quit being Virgil James." The last sentence was raspy and spoken in a low tone.

Tears filled Jo's eyes. She remembered

her parents and knew they felt the same way about each other. Her parents had died together so they never felt the extreme loss Paul obviously did. For that she was grateful.

Sam must have seen the emotion surging through her. He moved closer and wrapped his arm around her shoulder without saying a word.

"Thank you, Paul. I know this can't be easy." Jo slipped her arm around Sam's waist and leaned into him.

"It's all right. Martha has been gone for nearly ten years. She'd want me to help our daughter-in-law." He glanced at Jo and held her gaze. "She'd have been so happy to finally have a daughter, and the grandchildren that will come down the road. I wish she could have gotten to know you."

"I wish that, too." Then Jo added with a smile. "I would have liked to meet the woman who could keep you two corralled."

Sam chuckled. "That she did. She always made us mind our manners in her house. Never took any guff off of us either. She ruled the roost and we were happy to let her."

"Smart woman," said Jo, pointing

toward a stall where a horse waited. "Are you ready to go? I don't want Jackson to get away."

"I'm ready," said Paul. "I think it best if I check these places out alone and then come back to you with a report. I don't expect to actually find him, but I do hope to gather information. If I were him, I wouldn't stay in any one place too long."

"That was how I caught him last time. He made one of the saloons his 'home'," said Jo. "I don't think he'll make the same mistake again, but let's go find out."

"You can't be associated with us," said Sam. "We'll leave first and you follow in a while."

Paul nodded and walked over to the second stall which held a big black stallion.

"I just bought this stallion yesterday." Paul petted the nose of the large horse. "No one in town knows this animal."

"Perfect," said Sam

Jo watched Paul saddle the black. "Do you think he'll find him?" she whispered to Sam.

Sam took her arm and turned, walking with her out of the stable. "If anyone can, he can. He's been out of the life for a long time, but the things you learn never leave you. He'll find him. We just have to wait."

Grimacing, she looked up into his eyes. "Patience has never been one of my virtues."

CHAPTER 9

The first place Paul checked was the Nugget saloon—one of the seedier establishments in town, it served as a whorehouse, too. Folks in the place looked up at his entrance and the place got quiet, but the silence didn't last long. He was new and a little different than the regular clientele, but not enough to stop the music for long.

He walked back through the tables where men sat and a few girls wandered serving drinks. Some of the women sat on laps encouraging the customers to drink more of the watered-down rot gut. At some of the tables games of faro or poker were being played

When he reached the bar, Paul ordered a whiskey.

The barkeep set a shot glass in front of Paul and filled it from a bottle the bartender kept readily at hand.

"Where you from stranger?"

"Here and there. Lookin' for a man. About this tall," Paul raised his hand about shoulder height. "With bright red hair."

"Can't say I seen anyone like that," The bartender wiped out a glass with a grimy rag.

He didn't look up and Paul knew the man was lying.

Paul put a dollar on the counter. "Does this jog your memory any?"

The man squinted at the silver coin. "Four more of those might."

Paul pulled back the coin and set a five dollar bill in its place.

The man behind the bar picked up the money. "He and his friend were in here two days ago. They both had girls. Your man took up with Fancy, the redhead over there."

He jutted his chin at a voluptuous woman with a tray in her hand.

"The other man, brown haired and mean, took Daisy and beat her up some." He narrowed his eyes. "Gave her a black eye and a split lip. She won't be working except here in the saloon until it heals. He's not welcome back."

"Any idea where they went?"

"Fancy told me they were leading some bounty hunter on a merry chase through the countryside before coming back to town. He wanted to be caught by the bounty hunter, because she didn't know he had a partner. That's what he said—'she'. The man scratched his stubbly chin. "Never heard of a female bounty hunter before. That's all I know. They ain't been back since."

"Thanks friend. I'm takin' a room at the Hope's Crossing Hotel. If they come back, I'd appreciate you lettin' me know." Paul threw another five dollars on the bar.

"Sure will, mister. I sure will."

Paul left the establishment, the whiskey untouched

*****

Paul rode down to Sam and Jo's home and situated the horse in their barn, so it wouldn't be seen. Then he walked into the kitchen.

Jo turned and furrowed her brows. *Something went wrong, I know it did.* "You're here sooner than we thought you'd be. Sam went to work figuring we wouldn't hear from you until this evening."

"First stop was pay dirt. I thought it might be. The Nugget has a reputation for attracting the dregs of society. Cheap liquor and cheaper women."

Jo stopped scraping the dishes and wiped her hands on a towel hooked over the door of the cupboard under the sink.

"So don't keep me in suspense, what did you find out?"

Frowning, Paul shook his head. "I should wait until Sam gets here. How about a cup of coffee."

He was hedging. There was something he didn't want to tell her.

"Come on, Paul, he's my bounty, mine to find and bring in. My family is the one he murdered."

Paul nodded.

"He was there two nights ago. Took up with a redhead named Fancy. Seems funny him being a redhead that he'd take a redheaded woman. Although I saw her and she's built like a brick shit house. Sorry. I shouldn't have said that to you."

She shrugged. "I've heard worse. Go on."

Jo was anxious. So much so, she almost forgot her manners.

"I'm sorry, Paul. You wanted a cup of coffee didn't you? How about some sugar cookies to go with the drink? I'm afraid one side of them got a little too dark, I didn't turn the pan soon enough, but they still taste all right."

"Thanks, I'd appreciate that." He sat forward and leaned his elbows on the table. "I don't get somebody else's cooking' very often. I manage to fry up a steak now and again, and I'm good with eggs and bacon. But I don't bake at all."

"From now on I expect you to come have dinner with us. You're family and you belong here."

Paul flushed at her words. "Thank you, Jo. I appreciate the offer. But—"

At that moment, Sam walked in the door. "No buts about it, old man. Jo is right. It's time the world knows that you're my father. I'm not ashamed of you."

"I never thought you were. The charade was in case someone found out who I am…who I was."

Sam waved his hand. "Doesn't matter now if they do or not."

Paul was silent for a moment. "Well, all right then. I'd be pleased to join you all for dinner."

Jo smiled and walked to the older man. Now that she paid attention or maybe because she knew they were related, she saw that Sam and Paul had the same coffee-brown eyes with glints of gold that showed when they were amused or angry. In Sam's case, the gold was there when he was feeling amorous, too. Looking at Paul, she saw what Sam would look like in thirty years and the appearance was good. Paul was a handsome man.

She gave him a hug. "I'm pleased. Thank you, Paul. May I call you, Dad?" Her gaze dropped to the floor. "It's probably too soon for that."

Paul reached out, as his son had done so many times, and lifted her chin with a knuckle. "I'd be very happy if you called me, Dad. Nothing would make me happier."

Jo grinned, happy to be part of a family again.

Paul smiled.

*****

They sat at the kitchen table and Paul told them what he'd learned at the Nugget so they could decide what to do. The plan wasn't too hard to follow. Sam decided he would look for Jackson in the countryside. There were sure to be signs he left specifically for Jo.

Paul would continue checking the different establishments to see if Jackson had frequented any of them and hope to gain more information.

As for Jo, the men were united that she would stay home and be safe. That was why she decided to sneak out of the house and leave without telling Sam. He wouldn't like it, but Jackson was her bounty. She had to catch him. She had to confront him. *She had to finish this*.

About two o'clock in the morning, Jo rose from bed and walked to the spare bedroom. She'd left her clothes there so she wouldn't awaken Sam while she dressed. After that, she went to the kitchen, packed some food and filled her canteen, which she had stashed in the pantry.

Finally ready, she looked back toward her bedroom and whispered, "I love you

Sam Longworth."

Jo walked out the door toward the barn to saddle Smokey. When she was done, she led him out of the barn and closed the doors quietly behind her. Then she mounted and walked the horse to the next block trying to keep the sounds she made to a minimum. When she was sure she was far enough away, she kicked Smokey to a gallop and rode out of town heading west.

She left town at the same location where she'd lost Jackson a few days ago. He wanted her to find him and that was the best place to start.

Jo didn't want to have to explain to her husband. He just didn't understand. She had to do this. Finish this thing between her and Jackson. Billy Jackson was not getting away. He knew it and so did she. She'd either kill him this time or he'd kill her. Either way this would end, but she couldn't have Sam involved. She loved him too much to risk losing him. It was odd, the warm feeling she got when she admitted she loved Sam. Now if he would just admit the same thing to her.

*****

Sam woke early. Something was wrong.

He reached over to Jo's side of the bed. It was empty…and cold. She'd been gone for a while. He hoped she couldn't sleep and was having some chamomile tea to relax.

He went to the kitchen but Jo wasn't there. Cold fear gripped him. Jo was gone. In that instant, he knew she'd gone after Jackson, after Sam had expressly forbidden her to do so. When he found her, after he made sure she was all right, he wanted to put her over his knee. He wouldn't but he wanted to. He stopped for a moment. What had he done? By forbidding her to go, he'd forced her to take this drastic measure. Orders didn't work well with a woman like Jo. She'd push against that kind of demand every time.

Besides, the fact Jackson had murdered her family made him special. He wasn't just any bounty for her. The bounty money didn't even matter. What mattered was that she got justice for her loved ones.

Sam ran his hands through his hair turned, went back to the bedroom and dressed. If he was lucky, she only had an hour or so head start and he'd catch her quickly. Unfortunately, it wasn't quite daybreak yet, and he needed the light to follow her tracks. He lit a lantern. He guessed the direction she took was west, farther into the wilderness. But Jackson could just as easily be headed toward Bozeman.

*****

Jo dismounted and took the lantern with her to check the prints on the ground. Tracking at night was difficult at best and impossible at worst. Now was the worst. She knew that Jackson had hitched up with Frank Bauer. There were two sets of tracks she'd been following. Now she couldn't see either of the two in the rocky terrain she was in. She'd have to stop and make camp. Getting a couple of hours rest wouldn't hurt her or Smokey.

She unsaddled Smokey and hobbled him so he couldn't wander off. Then she used the lantern to find a fairly flat spot and set the saddle there. She was having a cold camp, no fire, because she didn't attract unwanted attention. Using the saddle as her pillow, she lay on the dirt with her blanket under her body. The ground was cold and she needed the insulation. Her coat was warm, she'd be fine for a couple of hours. She left the horse blanket on Smokey so he'd be comfortable, too.

She thought about the baby she was sure she carried. Jo knew she should tell Sam, he'd be thrilled. He'd also refuse to let her put her life in danger.

The morning sun hit her in the face and woke her. She stood immediately, stretched and then picked up the saddle and swung it up onto Smokey's back and tightened the straps to make sure the thing wouldn't fall off. Smokey wasn't a bloater, so she didn't have to make him blow to get the saddle tight. From nearby came the trickle of a stream flowing over rocks. That was good, both she and Smokey could use water. She walked him down to the creek where they both drank their fill and she refilled her canteen.

She finally found the tracks again. Jackson was headed to Bozeman. At least, that was the direction he took now. After leaving town on the west side, he'd circled toward the northeast. Maybe he was leaving, but she didn't think so. Jo figured he was leading her away from Hope's Crossing and Sam, so he could kill her. She was ready for that possibility and now she also knew that he had help, so she was forewarned.

Before she left the campsite, she made a sign for Sam so he'd know which way she went. She drew a heart with an arrow through it pointing out the direction she was taking—the third of these signs she'd left. The first had been at the edge of town where she started following Jackson. The second she'd left when Jackson made his turn toward Bozeman.

She didn't know when he'd awaken to find her gone, but she knew he'd follow her as quickly as he could. The heart and arrow seemed an appropriate symbol to lead him to her, especially now that she was expecting. If Sam had known that he'd have tied her to the bed to keep her safe.

Even though she knew she'd catch hell when he found her, she wanted Sam to find her quickly. She'd need his help to take down Jackson and his cohort.

Jo traveled through the countryside. Rolling hills with deep gully's and dotted with pine trees. Not a lot of places for an ambush, but she spotted a few. She wasn't familiar with the country, having only been there for about six weeks. Jackson may have been here for a shorter number of weeks, but he had more time to explore, as he didn't have a husband to care about.

*****

Sam found the heart with an arrow through it on the west side of town. Jo was leaving him signs. He followed the tracks on the trail toward Nevada City until he saw another heart. This time the arrow was pointing toward Bozeman.

He didn't like it. Jackson was leading Jo on a merry chase. At this rate, he'd be back in Hope's Crossing before night-fall. Sam followed the trail and came to another heart. He dismounted and inspected the ground. This one was at a camp spot. He saw where she'd hobbled Smokey. All the grass in that small area was eaten down. If not for that he wouldn't have known it was a campsite. There was no fire pit, no indication of pine boughs being made into a bed. Jo had a cold camp.

His pretty little wife was a good hunter, for bounties or anything else. She appeared to know how to take care of herself. Sam wasn't real sure how he felt about that. How he felt about not being needed. He kicked a rock with the toe of his boot, though it didn't help him feel better.

Sam remounted and took off in the

direction Jo had indicated. Jackson's trail gave the appearance he was headed to Bozeman, but the man was crafty. No telling where he actually was. For all they knew, he could be behind Jo and not ahead of her. Hopefully they didn't know Sam was on their trail as well. Jackson may have a partner, but so did Jo.

CHAPTER 10

Jo saw the camp about one hundred yards ahead. Jackson wasn't making any efforts to hide, not with a fire the size of a small building. She circled around the camp and checked for accomplices without finding any. Cautiously, guns drawn, she entered the site where she saw Jackson sitting on a fallen tree and stirring the fire.

"Come in, Jo." Jackson said without looking up.

"What are you doing here Billy? You know I'm not letting you get away. You have to go back to jail, so why are you letting me in. Where's your partner, Frank

Bauer?"

"Found out about Frank, did you? Well, it doesn't matter. He'll be along shortly."

Billy finally looked up and smiled. "Why here he is now, right behind you."

Jo felt the cold hard steel jab her back and dropped her Colts. Damn she was getting slow. Concentrating so hard on Billy, she hadn't heard Frank behind her. She hoped Sam wasn't too far behind her. His help would be very welcome right about now.

"Ah, the infamous Frank Bauer. You have quite the bounty on your head. Five hundred dollars, dead or alive. You better hope Billy doesn't decide to turn you in for the reward."

"Nah, I'm not worried. Billy's reward is double mine and he's better known. I'd have an easier time turning him in and he knows it. Besides, me and him are friends and you don't double cross a friend."

She snorted. "You obviously don't know Billy Jackson very well. He double crossed every member of his gang before I got to him."

Jo felt the gun in her back waver for a moment. Frank didn't know that about Billy.

Good, she'd planted the seed of doubt.

"That true?" Frank asked.

"She's a bounty hunter." Billy stirred the coals with the long stick he held. "She'll say whatever she needs to in order to drive a wedge between us."

Frank moved his gun from Jo's back but kept his hand on her shoulder so she wouldn't move without him knowing. "You didn't answer the question. Did you double-cross your gang?"

Billy lifted his head and stared right at Bauer.

"So what if I did? I figured I could get another gang if I was out but not if I was in."

"I don't like people who aren't loyal to their friends." Frank lifted his gun and pointed it at Billy.

Billy didn't wait for an invitation to shoot. He pulled his weapon and fired at Frank but missed.

Sucking in a breath, Jo dove to the ground and rolled away, hands around her waist to protect her child, while they shot at each other. Billy fired again and hit Frank in the leg.

Undeterred, Frank fired at Billy.

This time, the bullet hit his firing arm.

Uttering a groan, Billy dropped his Colt and dove for the bushes.

Now Frank had his gun trained on Jo.

"You think you've won don't you, girlie? But you haven't."

Jo closed her eyes while he leveled his gun. She thought of Sam and the wonderful life they could have had. The baby she carried.

A shot rang out.

Gasping, Jo opened her eyes. Shouldn't she hurt? Had he missed? She gazed over at Frank.

The outlaw was dead, his eyes still open in surprise where he lay sprawled on his back.

She heard the footfalls of a horse approaching and looked up into Sam's handsome face, now filled with fury.

He slid off the horse with the ease born of riding long hours and came over to Jo.

"What the hell did you think you were doing?"

"Sam, Jackson is still here." Jo grabbed at his hand to pull him down and pointed to the bush she'd seen Jackson dive into. "Don't worry about me. Find him."

Sam walked carefully to where Jo had

indicated, his gun drawn and ready.

He holstered his weapon. "No one is there. I can see where he was, but he's run off…again. And there's no more searching for you."

Out of habit she squared her shoulders and jutted her chin. "I can take care—"

He spread his arms wide, palms up. "Obviously, that's not true, since I just saved you from having your head blown off."

Jo dropped her gaze to the ground. No doubt existed that he had indeed saved her life. Bauer had been ready to shoot her and very nearly had. She owed Sam now.

"I do admit I owe you my life."

"I don't want you to risk your life for scum like Jackson. He's alone now. Catching him will be easier."

"Unless he goes to ground." Jo brushed the dirt from her arms, took off her coat and shook it to remove the dirt and weeds acquired when she hit the ground.

Sam braced his hands on his hips. "He wants you too much for that. He'll come at you again. Pick up your Colts, and let's go home. We've done all we can do here for now."

Knowing she heard the truth, Jo pointed at Bauer, thinking of the bounty to be claimed. "What about him?"

"His horse has got to be around here somewhere close."

They searched and found the animal in a clump of trees about fifty yards from camp. Sam led the buckskin mare back to the site and tied Hank Bauer's body over the saddle.

"Are you collecting the bounty, Sam? Because if you're not, I am. Five hundred dollars, dead or alive."

"How do you know what he's worth?"

"I check the wanted posters every time I bring lunch to you at the jail." She shrugged. "Old habits die hard."

"I'm not collecting it, because I'm the sheriff in Hope's Crossing, but you can."

"Thanks. I appreciate that. We'll put the money to good use. I want to add a bathroom and maybe another bedroom or two."

Sam frowned. "The house is big enough for us."

"But hopefully our family won't always be just two people." She wanted to tell him she was pregnant but he'd do something crazy, like forbid her again to find Jackson.

So she kept quiet.

"I don't want you chasing after Jackson."

Exactly what she'd thought. "Look, Sam, he won't kill me—"

"Are you crazy? Of course he'll kill you. That's why he came here."

Jo took a deep breath. "Let me finish. He won't kill me, because I'm not the only one who's after him now. It's us." She gestured between them. "You and me. We can capture him and you can make sure I don't do anything stupid."

Sam closed his eyes for a moment and then, he gave a curt nod. "All right. The two of us will go after Jackson, but if I think there is any chance that you could be injured, I'll pull you out and send you home. Agreed?"

A small thrill seized her. He was conceding. "What you think is dangerous and what I do are two different things, so if I agree with you, I'll go home on my own. Is that agreeable?"

Jo watched Sam close his eyes, pinch the skin above his nose and take a deep breath. She knew he didn't like not being in control but her daddy didn't raise a stupid girl or a cowardly one.

He looked over at her. "Why are you being so obstinate about this?"

"Because if I back down now, I'll lose myself and all I've worked to become. I'm not just Mrs. Sam Longworth. I'm Jo Shafter, bounty hunter and a darn good one. I don't want to be just one or the other. I need to be both, at least until Jackson is dealt with. I have to see him brought to jail or dead. I have to get justice for my parents and my brother before I let you and I become the family I know we can be."

His mouth pinched into a line, Sam nodded. "I understand and I'm letting you do that, get justice."

"Letting me?" Her body stiffened. Jo couldn't believe her ears. "You're letting me?"

"Perhaps that was not the best choice of words." Sam raised his hands and back pedaled for a moment. "I'll help you capture Billy Jackson. Then I'm asking that you turn in your buckskins and become just my wife and mother to our children."

"When we have children, I'll be thrilled to be their mother and that will become my most important job. Until then I'm your wife *and* a bounty hunter."

Sam shook his head.

"I don't like it, Jo. I don't like it at all. I want you home and safe."

Jo stepped around Frank's body and closed the distance between her and Sam, then took his hand. "Sam, as long as Jackson is free, no one is safe, least of all me. I'm the one he wants to kill. I'm the reason he's here in Hope's Crossing to begin with."

Sam squeezed her hand. "Let's go home. No telling where Jackson is now. I would bet he's high tailed it back to town or maybe on to Bozeman."

Jo nodded. "Hope's Crossing is the most likely. He won't go to Bozeman. Not with that wound. He'll have to find a doctor quick. Did you see my markers for you?"

Sam chuckled and lifted an eyebrow. "Hearts pierced with arrows? Were you trying to tell me something? Like maybe you love me?"

"Don't be ridiculous. I refuse to fall in love you with Sam Longworth. I reject being in love with someone who can't love me back."

Sam sobered, his eyebrows wrinkling..

"If I could love you, I would. Those

kinds of feelings are just not in me anymore, Jo. I'm sorry."

"Don't be." She turned toward her horse, Smokey, so that Sam wouldn't see her tears. "Just don't expect something from me that you're not willing to give."

"So be it."

"Yes," she said her heart breaking. "So be it."

*****

They arrived back home with no further contact with Jackson and no conversation with each other. In silence, they cared for the animals and went into the kitchen.

Sam was mad, and Jo was madder. He refused to even contemplate the possibility that he could love her. How was she supposed to make a family that way?

"Jackson has got to find a doctor somewhere. Frank Bauer shot him in his right arm. That's his gun hand and he couldn't hold the weapon after being shot."

They entered the kitchen and Sam sat at the table, while Jo lit the burner under the coffee pot.

Jo gave the information without looking at Sam. She would have to learn to get by without him. She couldn't stay where no possibility of love existed. She couldn't raise a child in that environment. A child should be surrounded by parents who not only love the child but love each other. The child she carried would know unconditional love from her, without Sam.

"Which is why he'll go for an ambush."

She started and looked to her side. "Huh? Wha...what?"

Sam stood over her with the coffee pot, ready to pour her a hot cup of coffee. "Jo, haven't you been listening?"

"No. Sorry I've got some other things on my mind."

"What could be more important than this?" He set the pot back on the stove.

"Nothing. I know that losing his gun hand because of this injury, makes an ambush more likely."

"Yes, you've got to be careful. I want either me or Dave with you all the time, whether you're here or walking around town."

She huffed out a breath. "There you go again."

Sam gestured surrender with his hands. "What did I do now?"

"You're assuming that I will let one of

you escort me all the time. You're telling me what to do and I don't like it."

Sam pinched the skin between his eyes. "Why can't we accompany you? We'd just make sure you're safe."

"You couldn't stop yourself from interfering."

"If you mean keeping you from getting shot or worse, then you're right. I intend to interfere."

"Why would you care?" Jo walked into the living room and Sam followed. She looked around wanting something to throw at him. Sam didn't have bookshelves, just the blue damask sofa, two large overstuffed chairs upholstered in a paisley blue material and the dark wood tables. A low one in front of the couch and tall ones beside each chair. Where were the books so she could chuck one at him? "We need bookshelves in here."

"Why? So you'll have something to throw at me?"

Jo stared at him wide-eyed. "How'd you know?"

He grinned. "You're a volatile woman. I see you looking all around the room. I'm not stupid, Jo. I can put two and two together and I'll leave the room just the way it is. I don't have any desire to get hit in the head by a flying book when you're angry."

Jo wanted to stamp her feet in frustration but that would be unseemly, even for her.

"Fine. I won't throw anything at you, but you still don't need to accompany me everywhere. We'd stand out like a sore thumb." She decided to take a different approach. "Look, Jackson won't ambush me at the places I'll frequent in town. He can be seen. He won't risk it, not with you here. He'll want me somewhere alone, and I'm not stupid enough to leave town without you." She grimaced. That was exactly what she'd just done.

Sam stood, hands on his hips. "What if he has me trapped, like he did your father?"

"Then neither Hell nor high water will keep me away so you might as well save your breath."

"Doggone it, Jo. That's exactly the problem. No matter what he says, you can't go alone with him. Billy Jackson is not a man to be trusted."

"I, of all people," she snapped and turned away. "Know how far I can trust him, which is not at all. You know that."

"That doesn't mean I don't worry."

"So you…uh…worry about me?" At his words, warmth invaded her chest. She twirled the end of the long braid that fell over her shoulder.

Sam cocked his head to the side and then back to the front. "Yes, I told you, I care about you. I don't want to see anything happen to you."

Could his caring turn into love? I can work with that, can't I? Make him realize that he loves me, because I must believe that he does or I can't stay. I won't be with a man who can't love me. Married or not.

Jo took a deep breath, cleansing away the doubts…for now. "All right. If I'm going out, I'll get one of you to come along. Fair enough? I really don't need you under foot here at home."

"Fine." His frown eased. "Only when you go out."

Billy Jackson wouldn't show his face with Sam or Dave escorting her everywhere, but maybe that was best. He'd have to come to her…at home, and she had no doubt he would come…just as soon as he was able.

CHAPTER 11

Billy waited for the doctor to arrive. Apparently, this man coming was the only doctor in town, so Billy would have to make him understand that if he talked about Jackson to anyone, he would die.

The old man with a shuffling gait, walked in. As he got closer Billy saw that he wasn't an old man, but he sure did look old. His hair was silver and messy, sticking straight out in places, like he'd just gotten out of bed. He wore round spectacles, and carried a wooden suitcase which he set on the floor next to the bed.

"Let me see your injury, young man, and

be quick about it."

The doctor was straight forward; Billy had to give him that. He turned and lifted his right arm so the doctor could see his gunshot, poorly bandaged with his handkerchief.

"I'm Doctor Kilarney. You can call me Doc. It looks like the bullet went through and missed the bone, but you've got two good-sized holes in your upper arm here. I'll treat them and then sew you up. That's all I can do."

"Go on ahead, Doc...hic. Do what you need...hic...to."

Doc pulled the bottle of whiskey off the night-stand and handed it to Billy.

"Take several swallows of this. It'll help with the pain. Then I'll give you some laudanum for later."

Doc Kilarney took the bottle and set it aside. He made Billy put his arm out straight and then the doctor grasped his wrist tightly before he proceeded to pour the liquor into the wounds, first the front side and then the back side without letting Billy go. The man was definitely stronger than he looked.

Billy howled. "Dammit Doc, what are you trying to do? Torture me?"

"I'm keeping your wounds from becoming infected. Now I'll stitch you up and bandage your arm. You should be back to using your hand in about ten days."

Pain throbbed over his wounds, and Billy spoke through gritted teeth. "Ten days! I need my hand sooner than that."

"You might be able to use it after seven days, but your grip will be weak and you could bust your stitches if you do."

Billy nodded. "I understand. I'll try to keep from using it."

The doctor sewed both bullet holes and then wrapped Billy's arm with cloth bandages from his case. He took out a small bottle of yellowish liquid.

"Place a few drops, no more than five, in water and drink it every three to four hours for the pain. I wouldn't try to do anything while you're on the laudanum. The medicine will dull your pain, but also dulls your senses." He cocked a gray eyebrow. "You'll be slow to draw and my guess is that a young man in your profession can't afford to be slow."

Billy held up his left hand and pointed his gun at the doctor.

"I don't have to be slow if the target is

standing right in front of me."

"Don't worry about me, young man. I'm not telling anyone you're here. I treat everyone the same. No one gets any information about one of my patients except the patient himself. If you want people to know where you are or anything else, you have to tell them, because I won't." His gaze narrowed. "Understand?"

Billy put the gun on the bed next to him.

"Yeah, Doc, I understand. Much obliged." He handed the silver-haired man a ten-dollar gold piece.

A grin flashed on Doc's mouth. "That's more than you need to pay, mister."

"Just a little incentive to keep this between us."

The doctor nodded. "Between us."

He closed his suitcase and stood holding it in one hand.

"Send Fancy for me if anything changes and you feel worse."

Billy lay back on the pillows and lifted his feet. "I will. Fancy, come take my boots off."

With a murmured farewell, the doctor let himself out.

Fancy bent over and tugged off one of

Billy's boots, then did the same to the other.

Both times showing Billy the cleavage he'd come to appreciate.

"Now get me something to eat and plan on staying all night."

"Sure thing, Billy."

She left and Billy was again alone. As always. He was best alone, but sometimes he needed comfort just like any other man, and Fancy was a pretty comforting gal.

*****

Two weeks had passed since Jo realized she might be pregnant. She'd missed one of her menses cycles and now she was missing her second, and was certain she carried Sam's child. She felt the urgency of settling this Billy Jackson case sooner rather than later. Once Sam knew she was carrying, he'd never let her out of his sight.

Jo poured a cup a coffee and took it to the table. She sat and heaved a huge sigh. What was she to do? She hated deceiving Sam, but until he realized that he loved her, she wouldn't tell him about the baby. Maybe. She didn't want him to say something he didn't mean, or for them to stay together just for the baby.

"That's an awful big sigh for someone

who assures me there's nothing bothering her."

Jo, with her back to the door, jumped at the sound of his voice and looked over her shoulder.

Sam stood in the doorway to the kitchen from the back yard.

Another instance of my weakening tracker skills. "What are you doing there? Spying on me?"

"I'm not spying. I'm checking all the entries into the house to make sure they are secure. Having this door standing open does not put my mind at ease. I could have been Jackson."

Jo rolled her eyes. "Jackson's healing somewhere. He won't be coming for me anytime soon."

"Nearly ten days have passed since we last saw him. If the bullet didn't hit a bone and break his arm he could be nearly healed. And you do admit he'll be coming for you, and this," he pointed at the door, "is not the way to remain safe."

He slammed the door closed and turned the lock.

"I didn't have these fancy locks installed on the doors for decoration. They are for you to use, to keep you safe."

"All right." He was probably right but she'd be danged if she was telling him so. "I'll start using them. Does that make you feel better?"

"A little." He ran his hand behind his neck. "Look Jo, I know you think I'm being a dictator about this but your safety is important. I don't need to bury another wife."

Hearing the gruffness in his voice, Jo stood and walked to him then wrapped her arms around his neck. "I don't want you to either. I promise I'll be careful and I'll wear my gun all the time." She reached up, knocked off his hat and mussed his hair. "Now kiss me and then go back to work."

Sam put his arms around her waist and gently pulled her close. His lips closed on hers and she answered his call. Within seconds, she was lost exploring their sensual heat. When they parted, both were breathing hard.

"I don't know how you do that. Each kiss is better than the last," Sam whispered as he caught his breath.

"I only do what you've taught me. So, if you like my kisses, it's because you don't hold anything back, so I don't either."

"You are amazing, wife."

Jo laughed and pulled out of his embrace. "So I am. Now you go to work, so I can get my chores done."

He released her, ran his hands through his hair to straighten it, then put on his hat and left the kitchen.

Jo smiled until she was sure he was gone, and then her smile faded. She had to find Billy Jackson, now. Jo wanted all this behind her so she could concentrate on her new life. She held her hand on her stomach. When would she start to show? She'd better go see Dr. Kilarney. He looked a bit eccentric but he was the only doctor in town. She wondered if he'd treated Jackson. Probably. Time to talk to the old man.

*****

Later that same day, Jo knocked on the door to the doctor's office.

"Come in, come in."

"Dr. Kilarney?"

The man was disheveled, like he'd slept in his clothes and his hair was wild, uncombed. A weariness weighed on him that had nothing to do with age. Looking closely at his face, Jo didn't see the wrinkles she thought she ought. Eccentric didn't begin to describe him.

"Yes, I'm Kilarney. What can I do for you, young woman?"

"I'm Jo Longworth, Sheriff Sam Longworth's wife. I think I'm pregnant."

The doctor straightened when Jo mentioned Sam.

Was that fear? Did he know something?

"Well, let's get you up on the table there." He pointed at the table in the center of the adjoining room. "And I'll check you out. How many of your menses have you missed?"

"Two. The second cycle was supposed to start a week ago."

The doctor checked Jo.

"Well, the good news is you are pregnant and based on your last menses, you're due in January."

Jo's heart leapt and she grinned. "Thank you, doctor. I'd appreciate it if you wouldn't tell Sam."

"You're the second person this week I've had to assure that I wouldn't discuss a patient with anyone else."

"Oh, I wouldn't have thought many people needed to make use of your discretion."

He smiled. "More than you can imagine, and for every reason under the sun."

"So if I asked you if this other person was a man with bright red hair, suffering from a gunshot to his right arm, you wouldn't be able to tell me that you saw him or where you saw him." She watched his face for a reaction. "Is that right?"

The doctor stiffened at her description of Jackson. "That's right."

Fighting back a smile. "Thank you, Dr. Kilarney. You've been very helpful."

"You're welcome. Don't forget to come in for regular checkups. I want to make sure this little one is doing well."

Jo stood and extended her hand. "I intend to. How much do I owe you?"

The man shook her hand.

"That'll be two dollars for today, and for each subsequent visit."

"Your fee is quite reasonable. Especially considering you're the only physician in town."

"I wish to make sure everyone can afford me. Now, do you have any other *medical* questions?" He waved a hand toward the door. "I do have work to do."

"Oh…uh…no, I don't have any other questions. Thank you for your time."

"You should tell Sam. He'll be happy to know he's becoming a father."

"I intend to, just not right away. How long until I begin to show?"

Doc tapped a finger on his chin. "You've probably got a month."

"I guess I better get what I need to do done by then."

"Yes, I guess you better."

Jo took her leave and hurried back home. The heat was almost oppressive and she was sweating by the time she reached the house. Sam would insist on knowing where she went if he caught her and while she wasn't ready to tell him she didn't want to lie.

When she got home, she immediately began preparing lunch. About an hour later, Sam and Dave walked into the kitchen from the living room.

"I'm glad to see you're using the locks." Sam bussed her cheek.

She stopped him and wrapped her arms around his neck.

"You know I care for you, don't you?"

Sam smiled. "Yes, I know you love me."

"*Care* for you." Her brows dipped into a frown. "I didn't say anything about love."

"Honey, with you women, it's all or nothing. You either love me, or you don't. There is no middle of the road. You can't just *care* for me. You love me."

She refused to acknowledge that he was right. She did love him, but she'd be danged if she'd tell him, knowing he would say he couldn't love her back.

"I won't argue in front of Dave, so just kiss me."

He kissed her. A real mind-numbing sort of kiss. The kind she wanted. Needed.

"Is that better?"

"Mmmm. Much."

Sam laughed and set her away from him. "What's for lunch?"

She rolled her eyes. Why was there always a question about food? "I made egg salad sandwiches. I've got to use up those eggs somehow. Besides, the filling was easy to make."

"Sounds good to me." He pulled out a chair. "What else?"

"What makes you think there is anything else?"

"You always make something for

dessert."

"I can see I've spoiled you. But you're right. I took the left-over biscuits from this morning and poured some canned peaches over them and I have clotted cream for the top."

"Mmm. My favorite. I don't think Dave has had that yet."

"No, sir, Boss." Dave rubbed his hands together. "But the dish sounds wonderful."

"It is," confirmed Sam. "It'll become your favorite, too."

Within ten minutes, the men finished lunch and both rubbed their full bellies.

"I've got to remember to make more egg salad when I do it for lunch. I'd hoped to have some left for dinner. Anything not to heat the house. I hadn't realized that June was such a hot month out here."

"Just wait until July and August," said Dave as he nodded his head. "That's when you'll wish you still had these cool times."

"Since I can't open the doors and get a breeze, I'd say it'll be miserable." She dabbed at her damp face with her apron.

"You can still open the windows," said Sam waving a hand toward the closest one. "They are small and high enough off the ground that Jackson will find it difficult to get in."

"Oh, thank you." She moved across the room and opened the window over the kitchen sink. Then she walked from the kitchen and opened the windows in the living room.

"I can already feel a little breeze. Do you feel it?" Sam raised his chin and closed his eyes, as the air moved past.

"Yes." Jo answered, as the air brushed her heated cheeks with wonderful coolness.

"You'll get more if you open the bedroom windows, too." Sam pointed out to her.

"I'll do that after you two go back to work," Jo shooed them out with her hands.

"Which is now. Come on, Dave, let's go," said Sam.

Jo walked to the door with the men grateful for the fresh air entering the house.

"Lock this after we leave. I'll be waiting until I hear the lock turn."

She did as he said and locked the door behind them. Then she went into their bedroom and opened that window. As she did, she thought she saw a flash of red hair by the barn, but she wasn't sure and couldn't leave to check or Sam would have her hide. He was probably still close by…she ran to the front door, unlocked it and saw that Sam was still in the front yard. He and Dave stood talking.

Nerves on edge, Jo ran out to him. "Sam. Sam. I think I saw him. Jackson. By the barn."

"Go back inside and lock the door."

She nodded, closed and locked the door. As much as she wanted Jackson, she found in only a few hours her priorities had changed. The confirmation that she was pregnant made her rethink her insistence that *she* get Jackson. As long as Sam brought him in, she could live with that. She had a babe to care for now. Someone who depended entirely on her. Someone she couldn't take chances with.

This changed everything.

CHAPTER 12

Jo leaned back against the locked door. Sam had to find him. Jackson couldn't be allowed to roam free. Sam was right, she needed his help. Now that Jo had another life to care for, she felt more cautious.

She paced the living room, waiting for Sam's return. Should she tell him? No, he'd place her under lock and key. Heck, she was already under lock and key. But she also knew she was the bait they needed for Jackson to show himself.

Jo needed a cup of tea. Something to help her settle down. She went to the stove, got the tea kettle and filled it with water. Uneasiness suddenly swept over her, made her turn cautiously around, the hairs on her neck standing on end.

Behind her, seated at the table with his Colt trained on her, was Billy Jackson.

"Hello, Jo. Nice to see you."

She was sorry to see that he was holding his gun with his right hand. He'd healed.

"I can't say it's nice to see you, Billy. I'd hoped you'd already gone to hell. Guess I'll have to send you there myself."

"That's big talk for someone staring at the business end of a gun."

"Harm me, and Sam will kill you, Billy. There's nowhere you can hide that he won't find you. He's a damn good bounty hunter."

She watched as color leached from Jackson's face.

"He's got to find you first. Let's go." He jerked his gun toward the door to the back yard.

Jo walked across the kitchen, followed by Jackson. She unlocked the door and opened it wide, hoping Sam would notice the open door right away.

"I saw you by the barn. Sam and Dave should be done looking for you by now and headed back. They'll catch us before you get fifty feet."

"No, who you saw was Fancy, not me. I saw Sam and his deputy go to the barn. She'll keep them busy for a short time while I get you out of here. I have horses stashed around the corner. Now move."

He'd gotten close enough to poke her in the back with his pistol. She decided she'd better go and try to stall later. She didn't want to get shot, especially not now.

Jo walked out the door and looked toward the barn. There was no one to be seen.

"Don't know what you're lookin' at. I told ya Fancy was keepin' them busy."

"Oh?" Without moving her head, Jo glanced toward the stables. "And how is she keeping them busy?"

"Well, see, she's hurt and needs their help."

"What did you do to her?" Jo couldn't keep the anger out of her voice. "I suppose she thinks she's in love and you used that against her."

"Yeah, she's in love with me." He chuckled. "Said I lead an exciting life. I told her she could join me if she did this one little thing. So she said yes. I just messed her up a little. She's pretending to hide from me.

A bit far-fetched, I know but your husband and his do-gooder deputy will fall for the ruse."

Jo couldn't believe her ears and clenched her fists. "She let you beat her up, just so she can go with you when you leave? That's insane."

"I never said she was smart or sane, now did I? No, Fancy is the kind of woman I need. She'll stand by me and help me in any way I want."

Jo stopped, a frisson of fear traveled up her spine, and turned her head to look at him. "You're sick, Billy. A sick, sick man."

His face changed, angry lines formed, his eyes narrowed and his mouth turned down. He again poked her in the back with his gun. "Get moving. Now."

She turned forward and continued walking in front of him. *Someone must be in the area. Surely if I made noise they would come, but would I survive the gunshot I would surely receive.* They went around the corner from the jail and there, behind a large lilac bush and out of sight, were two horses. One was a big, bay stallion and the other a piebald.

"Nice horses. Someone's got to have

seen them. Someone will put two and two together and point at you.'

"That's highly unlikely. I got these horses from an old miner who wanted to go home. Well, I sent him home. Now, put your hands out in front of you." He grabbed both her hands with his left, holstered his gun, took a length of rope from his pocket and tied her wrists together.

Fighting her growing apprehension, Jo struggled to keep her voice even. "My God, you killed a man for his horses? You've gotten really low, Billy."

He pulled his gun from his holster and pointed at the horse. "Get on that piebald and shut the hell up."

The horse, pretty with its bold black and white markings, was difficult for her to mount with her hands tied and he'd tied them tight. She could already feel her fingers tingling. Soon they would be numb and useless. In such a condition, she didn't dare try to out ride him, he could shoot her in the back and probably would. She had to figure out a way to let Sam know where she was, but she didn't know how.

*****

Sam and Dave entered the barn and saw

a red-haired woman, who clearly had been beaten. Sam approached her.

She was shaking so bad the gun pointed at him wavered wildly in her hand.

"Stay away from me."

"What's your name, girl?" Sam didn't think she was more than about seventeen or eighteen but age was hard to determine under all the makeup and with a black eye and split lip. "Did Billy Jackson do that to you?"

"Yes. Now stay away."

A chill ran over Sam's body. Jackson had set this up? "What?! Dave you stay here with her, I'll go back to the house." Moments later Sam saw the back door standing wide open and his worst fears were realized. Jo was gone. Billy Jackson had taken her.

Just to make sure he checked every room in the house. He ran back to the barn and walked directly up to Fancy.

Eyes wide, she lowered the gun.

Blood pounded in his ears and he grabbed her by the upper arms and shook her.

"Where is he? Where's he taking her?"

"I don't know. What makes you think I

know anything? He did this to me." Whimpering, she pointed at her face. "Why would I hide anything from you?"

"I know you're providing a distraction for him to get away. Otherwise you'd be at the doc's office not here. You probably think you're in love with him." He narrowed his gaze. "How wrong am I?"

Fancy's face turned white and her hand holding the gun between her and Sam, shook even more.

"Ever been to jail Fancy? Those conditions are not bad, but prison, that makes what you do for a living look like a walk in the park."

Sam took the gun gently from her hand.

"Don't cover for someone who would beat you up. You deserve better than that Fancy."

Blinking fast, she looked between the men and began to cry.

Sam handed her his handkerchief from his pocket.

Fancy dabbed her eyes. "He was supposed to ride out to the wooded area west of here toward Nevada City."

"I know the area you mean. Dave, take Fancy here to the doctor." He jerked his head to the side. "Tell him to put the fee on my bill. I'm going after Jo. They can't have gotten too far."

Sam got Smokey out of the stall and saddled him. "Smokey," he said to the horse as he worked. "You're faster than any other horse I know, and you love Jo like she loves you. We've got to find her."

When he was done, he mounted, kicked the horse into a cantor and flew through the open barn doors. He rounded the corner onto a less crowded side street that ran parallel to Main Street at a full gallop riding as hard and fast as Smokey could take him. The horse had stamina and a deep chest, he'd run a lot longer than any horse Jackson could have managed to get a hold of. Smokey was one of a kind in these parts, even stronger than Sam's own stallion.

"Out of the way!" Sam shouted to people crossing the street in front of him. "Get out of the way!"

They looked up and their eyes widened when they saw him coming but they moved. Within moments, he'd passed the town limits and was headed toward Nevada City. Getting closer, he could feel them just ahead. Smokey was catching them.

Sam crested the top of a hill, and as he did he saw Jackson with Jo at the bottom, just heading into Nevada City. He would catch him before Billy could take Jo out and kill her. He looked to be leading her horse by the reins, rather than give Jo a chance to get away. All Sam wanted was for Jo to be safe. He urged Smokey forward.

He knew the minute Jackson looked back at Jo and saw Sam gaining on them.

Jackson dropped the reins to Jo's horse and kicked his into a full gallop, thundering out of the small mining town toward the mountains. He could lose Sam there easily enough.

But Sam didn't care about Jackson now.

He pulled up beside Jo.

As soon as she saw him she burst into tears. Sam slid off Smokey and raised his arms toward her.

She leaned down into them, sure he would catch her.

He did then set her on her feet and quickly untied her hands.

As soon as she was free, she yelled as the blood rushed back in, causing her pain. Then she threw her arms around Sam's waist.

"Thank you for coming for me. Thank you for catching him. He would have killed me. I have no doubt he'll try again. He won't stop until I'm dead."

She buried her face into Sam's chest while he held her close, his arms wrapped tightly around her.

"Of course, I'd come for you. You're my wife. I…I care for you, you know that." He rubbed his hand up and down her back.

"But you don't love me. You could just get another mail-order bride." She knew she was being irrational and needy, but she really needed Sam to love her…to realize that he loved her. Jo knew he did, deep down where love really counted. She knew he did, but he hadn't realized that what he called caring was actually love.

"I don't want another mail-order bride. I want you. Dag-nab-it why can't you get that through your beautiful head?"

Jo stopped and blinked. "Thank you for wanting me."

Sam rolled his eyes, shook his head and smiled. "Yes. I want you and I care for you. Why do you think I can't keep my hands off you?"

"Well, I…I just thought it had been a

long time for you and that's why…" She lowered her gaze but hugged him tighter. "I…I care for you, too, Sam."

She felt rather than heard his laughter.

Then he let loose and pushed her away from him just far enough that he could look into her eyes.

"You love me, Jo. I've told you before, but you refuse to believe it."

She set her hands on her hips. "Just like you refuse to believe that you're in love with me. And you are. You can deny it all you want, but you came after me because you love me."

He frowned. "I came after you because you're my wife, and you're staying my wife."

Jo looked up into Sam's eyes. Angry eyes right now. Cold, dark eyes that only a moment ago were filled with laughter. She couldn't talk to him when he was like this. Instead, she wrapped her arms around him and got as close as she could. Sam was safe, and she needed to be safe.

Being pregnant had changed her. She'd never been one to cry at the drop of a hat or care if someone loved her or not. But now, being loved seemed so important, so much so she was contemplating leaving Sam because he said couldn't love her.

Jo was in such a quandary. She couldn't leave because she was pregnant and Jackson would come after her, She couldn't, wouldn't risk her child. On the other hand she couldn't stay because she was pregnant and Sam refused to love her. How could she raise a child in that environment? And then there was Paul. She knew he would be a doting grandfather. But parents should love each other, like her parents had. That's what she wanted for her child, what she grew up with. Two parents loving each other and the children.

Sam held Jo for a long time, but then he pulled back.

"Jo, we need to go home. Can you ride? Do you want to ride Smokey, or ride with me?"

"You please. I want to feel your arms around me on the way home."

That seemed to soften him some, and the anger eased from his features. "All right. Let me mount first, then I'll pull you up onto my lap."

In a few minutes, Jo was riding in front of Sam, his arms around her holding her safe. She rested her arms on top of his.

"What will we do, Sam? He'll keep coming, until one of us is dead, him or me. I want to make sure it's him. I have too much to live for."

"You don't sound like you did when you first came. You're more cautious now. Why? What's changed?"

"I've gotten settled and I like my life. I'm not willing to give that up. I like living where I do…with you. I'd like it even better if you realized that you love me, too."

"Ah ha, you admit you love me."

"Never." She ignored the error she'd made. "Not until you admit that you love me." She decided never to mention the subject again until she heard his admission.

He rested his chin on her shoulder and whispered in her ear. "Jo, I would if I could. Really. I want to love you, I just can't. That feeling is not a part of me anymore."

"You're just being stubborn and bull-headed." Jo slumped against him, pouting.

Sam chuckled. "Wishing you had a book?"

She smiled and then giggled. "Yes. As a matter of fact I am. I'm close enough to throw it at you and not miss."

He laughed. "Ah, Jo, you do please me."

"Well, that's nice to hear. But don't think you can make me forget what we were fighting about."

Sam sighed and tightened his hands on the reins.

When they arrived back at the house, Sam went directly to the barn.

He dismounted Smokey and held his arms up for Jo.

She leaned down, grasped his shoulders and let him catch her as she slid from the horse.

He led Smokey into a stall. "I want you with me so we'll go to the house together. I'm not taking the chance that he could have gotten in again."

"Fat lot of good the locks did. I don't know how he managed to get in, but it had to be through the kitchen door. He was sitting at the table, waiting." She shuddered, thinking about what could have happened if Sam hadn't followed her as quickly as he did.

Sam walked over to her and wrapped her in his arms.

"It's all right now. You're safe. I won't let anything happen to you."

How could she not tell him about the baby? Was it fair to him not to? No, but she was scared. What if she was wrong and he really didn't love her? Could she stay with him even then? But she wasn't wrong. She couldn't be. She had to tell him.

"Sam, there's something we need to talk about."

He heaved the saddle from Smokey to the saddle bar. Then he grabbed the comb and curried Smokey.

"What would that be?"

"Well, I…uh…I'm...uh—"

He glanced over his shoulder. "Spit it out, Jo. What's the problem?"

She sighed and rushed out the words. "I'm having a baby."

Sam's hand stilled. He dropped the curry comb, went to Jo, picked her up and swung her around "A baby! But that's wonderful."

"No it's not," she cried as she pushed against his hold. "Now put me down. Not with Jackson still on the loose it's not. I've changed my way of working because I'm afraid to get hurt, afraid to injure the child. How can I do my job if I'm feeling that way?"

"Jo, oh, honey." He leaned close to gaze

into her eyes. "Is this what you've been afraid of? Why you have to take care and haven't been chasing leads for Jackson?"

She nodded. "I can't risk the child's life. If it was just me, well, that's something else. But now that it's me and a child, and…I can't take the risk with their life."

"We'll get him, Jo. I promise you, *I'll* capture him. I don't want you to worry about this or anything else. You need to stay healthy for the baby."

"You see. I knew you'd say that. Now you'll try and protect me rather than tracking down Billy Jackson."

Sam stubbornly set his jaw.

"Who says I can't do both?

Jo cocked her head to one side.

"How can you protect me when I'm the bait you need to get Jackson to come out of hiding?"

"There's got to be some other way."

"There's not and you know it. Next time, I'll be ready for him. I'm not depending on you or anyone else for my safety. And certainly not on some fancy locks."

Sam reddened and resumed brushing Smokey.

"I'm sorry." Jo's anger at Sam dissipated. "I know you were only protecting me with the locks but they don't work or he's figured some way around them."

He shrugged. "I'll just stay with you all the time."

"You can't do that. You have a job and a town to protect."

"You come first."

"That's not how Billy Jackson will be caught. You have to let me be, or at least have it look like I'm unprotected."

"So how are we to do that?"

She slumped her shoulders. "I don't know."

CHAPTER 13

Four weeks had passed since Jo's harrowing escape from Billy Jackson. She thought about it every day. Her life had almost gotten back to normal.

She was cooking lunch for the men. making her famous, at least with Sam and Dave, chicken and dumplings. She walked into the jail with the Dutch oven full of the delicious offering.

"Here now," Sam quickly stood, went to her and took the pot from her. "You shouldn't be carrying that. It's too heavy."

Jo rolled her eyes,

Dave chuckled.

Sam had been this way since she'd told

him about the baby a month ago. Not letting her do anything. She'd gotten to where she rose in the middle of the night so she could clean the house. He finally stopped staying home so she was able to do her chores during the day, but he was being ridiculous.

"Sam, the doctor said I can do my regular chores until I'm at least eight months. I'm only three. You can start worrying about my carrying a pot then."

"Are you carrying your gun?"

"Yes, it's in the pocket I sewed in my dress. It can't be seen, obviously, or you would have known about it."

"Well, I worry and so does Dave."

"That's right Jo," agreed Dave as he filled his plate with the savory food. "We worry about you. One of us has an eye on the house all the time, but we can't see the kitchen door. You'll have to be on your guard."

"I've been telling her that every day," said Sam.

"I know and I have been," said Jo biting back the exasperation she felt. "I check every room before I enter. It's rather tedious process, but I remember when he got the drop on me. I won't let that happen again, if

I can help it."

"Glad to hear it," said Sam holding out his arms. "Now come and give me a kiss, then I'll walk you home."

"You don't have to walk me home."

"Ah, tired of me already." Sam clasped his hand over his chest as though he was broken-hearted.

Jo rested her hands on her hips. "You know that's not true."

"I'm just teasing."

Jo grinned. "So am I."

She stretched up and kissed Sam on the cheek.

He grabbed her around the waist, pulled her close and gave her one of his curl-the-toes kisses, as though Dave wasn't even there. Sam decided long ago that Dave was family and he'd kiss her however he wanted to in front of him, much to her embarrassment.

Jo shook her head when they parted. "You know what that does to me."

He lifted an eyebrow and gave her a cocky smile. "I know."

Sam circled his arm around her waist and led her out the door and to the house. He checked every room before he let her go in.

When she was alone again, Jo made bread and let it rise while she went to feed the animals. She stopped doing the feeding them in the mornings because she wasn't awake enough to be alert until later in the day, and she needed to have all her wits about her.

She walked to the barn and peered in through the door before entering. Jo pulled her gun and entered, checked the stalls, the tack room and found no one. She placed the gun back in her pocket.

Smokey was in his stall stamping and snorting.

Jo went over to him, opened the stall, and went in to soothe him.

"What's the matter, big guy, you miss me?"

"He probably hasn't, but I have."

Billy Jackson sat up from behind a hay bale, pointing his Colt at her.

"I've been waiting all morning for you, Jo, or even Sam, either one of you would be all right."

Fear roiled in her stomach as she turned slowly to face him. "Billy Jackson. I wondered where you'd gone. I was hoping you'd given up."

"That's what I wanted you to think. You'd get lax and I'd get my hands on you again."

"I'm not leaving with you, Billy." Jo stood her ground, spreading her legs just a little for support, and putting her hands down at her sides for easier access to her gun.

"But you are, only were not leaving town this time. I found me a nice little house on the other side of town." His grin barely showed teeth. "Should work fine for what I have in mind."

Moving slowly, Jo moved to her pocket and placed her hand around her Colt.

"I'm not leaving with you." She cocked her gun and coughed to cover the noise.

"I'll shoot you where you stand, if you don't go with me."

"Why would I leave just so you can kill me some place else? I know there is no way you let me live."

His eyes narrowed. "But I might let Sam live."

"Highly unlikely." She shook her head. "You blame him for getting in your way. You'll never let either of us live."

His chin jutted upward. "You're right I

won't, so I'll just take care of you now."

Jo aimed as best she could with her gun in her pocket and fired before Billy could.

The bullet hit him in his side and he jerked.

He shot but the bullet went over Jo's head.

Jo pulled her Colt from her pocket, dropped while protecting her belly and rolled, prepared to fire again.

Suddenly Smokey was there, between her and Billy, stomping on him, rearing and coming down again.

Billy screamed dropped his gun and put his hands over his head.

Smokey came down on Billy's legs.

Her back braced against the stall, Jo heard the crack of bones breaking.

"Call him off, call him off!"

Jo walked over and picked up Billy's gun. Then she whistled, and Smokey shook his head but came to her.

Billy was in bad shape.

Sam ran into the barn, gun drawn and went immediately to Jo.

"I heard shots. Are you all right?"

"I'm fine, but he's not doing so well." She pointed with her gun at Billy, who lay not moving.

"Is he dead?"

"I don't think so. Just passed out from the pain. He's shot in the side, and Smokey broke one or both of his legs and probably bruised his ribs. I should have known something was wrong when I came in. Smokey was acting skittish in his stall. He was warning me." Jo replaced her gun in her pocket, handed Billy's gun to Sam, and went to Smokey. "Yes, you're a good horse and a good friend, aren't you?" She petted him, kissed his nose, and scratched him behind the ears.

"I'd say he's earned an extra scoop of oats, wouldn't you?" Sam stood on the other side of the horse, petting him,

"Yes, and a couple of horse cookies, too." Jo looked down at the injured man. "We should probably send for the doctor. I don't think he's going anywhere under his own steam."

Billy was lying still on the ground, just starting to come around. He moaned in seeming agony and Jo didn't feel the least bit sorry for him.

They sent Dave for the doctor, who came right away.

"I didn't think this young man would live too long, given his life style. He picked off more than he could chew with you, Jo," said Doc Kilarney.

"I owe him more than just a few broken bones, but at least this time he won't escape before he gets to prison and gets hanged for what he did to my family."

"And he won't find prison a pleasant place especially with a broken leg."

Sam wrapped his arm around Jo's shoulder.

"Are you sure you're all right? I can see from your dress that you rolled on the ground and there's a hole in the skirt where you shot Billy from your pocket."

"I'm fine. I did drop and roll after I shot him, but I'm fine not even a scrape." Jo showed him her hands, which were dirty but unhurt.

Sam kissed each of her palms.

"I'm thankful you're all right. I don't know what I'd do if I lost you."

Jo sucked in a breath. She couldn't believe he'd said that. He had to love her to say that kind of thing didn't he? She wished she knew. Jo was so confused, but now wasn't a good time to make a decision about anything. She'd just had the second worst scare of her life, on top of being very emotional because of her pregnancy.

Sam and Dave made a stretcher for Billy and carried him back to the doctor's office. After getting bandaged and having his leg casted by Doc, Billy would be spending his days and nights in the jail. Dave would watch him during the day and Charley would take over at night, at least until they could arrange for transport back to prison in Illinois.

Sam returned home, walking through the waning light.

Jo was shaping bread dough into loaves for baking.

"You're amazing. After a scare like you had today, you're back to baking bread like it was any other day."

"Kneading helps work out frustrations."

"What are you frustrated about?"

She turned and leaned against the counter, her arms folded across her chest. Her hands, covered in flour, left marks on her bodice. "You. How can you say you don't know what you'd do without me and then insist that you don't love me? I don't understand. You actions make no sense."

"I loved one woman and she betrayed me. I vowed I'd never live like that again."

After all this time I don't know his wife's name. "Your wife, what was her name?"

"Mabel"

"Yes, Mabel, hurt you I don't deny that, but that is no reason to give up on love. If you can't find love with me, what about our children? Will you feel love for them?"

"Of course. They are children, part of me and you. I care so much for you, Jo. How could I not love them?"

Jo wanted to scream. No matter what she said, Sam wouldn't admit that his feelings were love. Would she accept that? Could she?

"I'm taking a walk. I'll be back after a while."

"Do you want me to go with you?"

"No, I need to think. I'll be back."

Sam nodded.

Jo walked all the way to the end of the boardwalk and back to the house. She couldn't come up with a solution that didn't involve her leaving because she couldn't live without love.

CHAPTER 14

A few hours later, Jo walked into the hotel.

Effie came around the desk to greet her with a hug.

"Are you sure you want to do this? Jo, maybe if you talked to Sam—"

"He's made his thoughts on the subject perfectly clear. He'll never love me. I need more Effie."

"Let me get you a room. I want you to be comfortable until the stage comes from Bozeman. You know how it is, the stage is never on time."

Jo shook her head, narrowing her gaze. "I know you, Effie Smith. You're trying to buy time so you can talk to Sam. It won't matter, but I do appreciate the room."

"You're right. I do want to see Sam."

Jo nodded, but her throat was too tight to speak. Was she on the right path or giving up a good man for a dream?

*****

Sam walked into the house and knew immediately something was wrong. The room was too quiet. No wonderful smells came from the kitchen. He walked quickly to their bedroom. The closet door stood wide open, and Jo's valise was gone from the floor. One glance at the closet told him only his clothes remained.

He went to the bureau and pulled open Jo's drawers. Empty.

Why had she left? Because he couldn't love her? Was it so important? He thought they had something special. Was that love?

Sam hurried to the hotel. That's where Jo had to have gone. There wasn't any place else she could go.

"Effie," he strode up to the counter where the little woman stood. "Where is she?"

"She doesn't want to see you, Sam."

"That's too bad." He stared down at the

small woman, his hands on the registration counter. "She owes me an explanation. Why'd she leave me?"

*****

Jo sat in the big overstuffed chair in front of the fireplace. This room was huge furnished with a big bed with dark wood head and foot boards, and a nightstand on either side of it. Across the room was the fireplace with a sofa and two large chairs in front of it, in one of which she now sat. Under the window was a small light wood table with two matching chairs.

A bureau and wardrobe also stood in the room and there was a private bath room with actual running water. All this opulence, and all she wanted was Sam. She couldn't care less about the amenities of the room. Without Sam the space was empty.

A knock sounded on the door.

Jo wiped her cheeks and hoped she didn't look too bad. Effie was probably checking on her and she didn't want the poor woman to worry.

She pasted on a smile and opened the door. Her smile faded. "Sam? What are you doing here?"

"I couldn't let you go without knowing

how I feel. May I come in?"

Jo stood to the side and let him pass in front of her. She closed the door behind him.

"If you're here to tell me again how much you care for me, save your breath."

"I've done a lot of thinking. I don't feel about you like I did Mabel and I wonder if what I felt for her was love. I deserve your reluctance to believe I've changed, but I have. I love you, Jo. I've always loved you, I was just afraid to say the words."

"And what makes you think I'll believe you?"

"You don't have to. You can tell me to leave and I will, but not until you believe that I love you and I will always love you. What I felt for Mabel and the feelings I have for you are so much different, I thought I must not love you. But I felt guilty about Mabel rather than loved her, because she died when she was leaving me. Even before that when we first married, it was guilt that kept me with her, not love."

Jo felt the tears run down her cheeks. Sam was making all of her dreams come true.

"I love you, too."

Sam took her in his arms and kissed her

thoroughly.

"You're mine Jo Longworth and I'm never letting you go."

"Oh, Sam."

She met his lips with her eager response.

Sam picked her up in his arms and carried her to the bed.

"Show me. Make love to me, Sam."

"With pleasure."

They didn't leave the room all day or all night, not even for meals.

Effie took pity on them and sent them a tray of cold offerings including chicken, biscuits, cheese and fruit, along with a pot of coffee and one of tea.

"Effie loves us, you know?" said Jo, popping a piece of cheese in her mouth before she picked up the tray off the table and moved it to the bed. "She made sure I took a room."

"I'm forever grateful to her."

Sam tore into a chicken leg and washed it down with some of the still hot coffee.

"So am I. I've never been more miserable in my life as I was at the thought of leaving you, but I couldn't stay with the way things were. You understand that now, don't you?"

"Yes. I want to be the most important person in your life, too."

"You are. That's why I was so torn up. But that is all behind us." Jo lay on the bed and looked down at her belly. With one hand, she rubbed circles on her stomach. "She's much happier, too."

"She?" He swallowed and glanced her way with a crooked eyebrow. "How do you know it's a she?"

"I just feel it. Five months from now she'll make her entrance. What shall we name her?"

"I think that we should be prepared with a boy's and a girl's name, just in case your woman's intuition is wrong."

"If you insist. I think we should name the girl Mary Martha, after our mothers and if by chance it's a boy, we name him Paul Rex, after our fathers. What do you think?"

Sam leaned down and kissed her tenderly.

"I think you're wonderful and I totally agree about the names."

Jo reached up, cupped his unshaven jaw and smiled. "Ah, Sam."

EPILOGUE

Five months later

"How long does a birthing take? She's been in there with the doctor for hours. Shouldn't the baby have come now?"

Sam paced the length of the room, stopped periodically and looked toward the bedroom, before pacing again. The doctor insisted he stay in the living room during the birthing, when every instinct in his body told him he needed to be with Jo.

"How can you be so calm?" he demanded of Paul.

"It's not my wife who's giving birth, now is it?" Paul sipped from his cup of coffee. "You should have seen me when you were born. I was a wreck for days, even after you were here safe and sound."

"Why?"

"Because you were so small. I was sure that I would drop you every time I picked you up. Yet somehow, you managed to survive…without any lasting damage, anyway." Paul chuckled.

An infant's cry came from down the hall.

Sam raced toward the sound. When he arrived, he stopped and took a couple of deep breaths before entering the room.

A disheveled Jo sat back on the pillows propped against the headboard. She held a swaddled form in her arms.

"Well, is it a girl like you were sure it would be?" asked Sam as he approached the bed.

Jo smiled and shook her head. "No, we have a beautiful boy, this time." She opened the blanket so Sam could look upon his new son. "Do you want to hold him?"

Sam put up his hands and shook his head. "No, not yet. I'm content to look upon him as you hold him." And look he did. He checked the baby's fingers and toes, counting to make sure there were ten of each. He ran his hand over his son's pale blond hair, so light the boy looked bald. "He takes after his mother."

"Only the hair." Smiling she ran a finger along Sam's cheek. "His eyes are brown like yours and I have a feeling he'll probably be as stubborn as you."

Sam chuckled. "He'll never *not* know what love is. We'll make sure he understands."

Little Paul started to fuss.

"I think he's probably hungry. Being born is hard work, believe me."

"I would imagine it is. I wanted to be with you, but Doc wouldn't let me."

"I know. I wanted you there too, but the experience wouldn't have been pleasant for you. I called you every name in the book."

Sam raised his eyebrows. "Why?"

"Because I decided during my pain, that this was all your fault."

"It took both of us."

"I didn't say they were rational thoughts, just that was what I felt at the time."

"Well, if you give me a beautiful bundle of baby each time you cuss me out, you can cuss me out as much as you want."

Glassy-eyed and smiling, she looked down at the baby and then back up at Sam. "Thank you."

"For what?"

"For giving me what I needed and not letting me leave. I would have been miserable. I love you so much."

"Your leaving is what made me realize how much I love you. I didn't understand the feelings I was having until I was confronted with not having you in my life."

"May I come in?"

Paul stood in the doorway, leaning against the door frame.

"Yes, come in and see your namesake before Jo feeds him."

Paul walked to the bed and smiled down at the baby and his mother.

"You did good, Jo. He's beautiful."

"Thank you. I'm so glad you like your grandson."

"Like him? I love him. He's part of my two favorite people, and he has the best name in the world."

He actually glowed, his pride evident.

"Do you want to hold him?" asked Jo.

"Of course."

He leaned down and plucked the baby from Jo's arms. The blanket was still open and he too counted all the baby's fingers and toes, touching each one. Then he rubbed little Paul's belly and tickled his feet.

Little Paul shoved his fist in his mouth and then took it out and wailed. It was more of a squeak but the sound got his point across.

"If you will excuse us, Paul," said Jo. "I need to take care of the little one's hunger."

"Of course." He handed the child back to Jo, bent and gave her a kiss, and clasped his son on the back. "You did well. He's a fine son."

"Thanks, Dad."

When her father-in-law had left, Jo opened her nightgown and helped little Paul find her nipple and take it. He first spat it out a couple of times, but then he latched on and began to suckle.

"Oh," said Jo in surprise.

"What?" Sam sat on the mattress. "What's the problem?"

"It's uncomfortable. Effie tells me that is not unusual to begin with. I'll get used to him suckling, and all will be fine."

"I wish I could take the pain away for you."

"Don't worry, sweetheart. Everything's fine. As a matter of fact, it's wonderful and I wouldn't change any of it, the good feelings and the bad, for anything in the world. Everything we went through brought us to this place and gave us this wonderful baby boy." Jo smiled down at her new son.

"I want you to know that I love you, Jo. I mean to tell you that every day. I don't want you to ever forget."

"Don't worry, I won't forget nor will I let you forget. I love you, too, more than I can ever show you."

"You just showed me in the best way possible. You gave me a son."

Sam sat on the edge of the bed and watched the two most important people in his life, his throat so tight he couldn't speak

This was his family, his joy…his life.

THE END

ABOUT THE AUTHOR

Cynthia Woolf is the award winning and best-selling author of fifteen historical western romance books and two short stories with more books on the way. She was born in Denver, Colorado and raised in the mountains west of Golden. She spent her early years running wild around the mountain side with her friends.

Their closest neighbor was about one quarter of a mile away, so her little brother was her playmate and her best friend. That fierce friendship lasted until his death in 2006.

Cynthia was and is an avid reader. Her mother was a librarian and brought new books home each week. This is where young Cynthia first got the storytelling bug. She wrote her first story at the age of ten. A romance about a little boy she liked at the time.

Cynthia loves writing and reading romance. Her first western romance Tame A Wild Heart, was inspired by the story her mother told her of meeting Cynthia's father on a ranch in Creede, Colorado. Although Tame A Wild Heart takes place in Creede that is the only similarity between the stories. Her father was a cowboy not a bounty hunter and her mother was a nursemaid (called a nanny now) not the ranch owner.

Cynthia credits her wonderfully supportive husband Jim and the great friends she's made at CRW for saving her sanity and allowing her to explore her creativity.

TITLES AVAILABLE

THE HUNTER BRIDE – Hope's Crossing, Book 1
GIDEON – The Surprise Brides
MAIL ORDER OUTLAW – The Brides of Tombstone, Book 1
MAIL ORDER DOCTOR – The Brides of Tombstone, Book 2
MAIL ORDER BARON – The Brides of Tombstone, Book 3
NELLIE – The Brides of San Francisco 1
ANNIE – The Brides of San Francisco 2
CORA – The Brides of San Francisco 3
JAKE (Book 1, Destiny in Deadwood series)
LIAM (Book 2, Destiny in Deadwood series)
ZACH (Book 3, Destiny in Deadwood series)
CAPITAL BRIDE (Book 1, Matchmaker & Co. series)
HEIRESS BRIDE (Book 2, Matchmaker & Co. series)
FIERY BRIDE (Book 3, Matchmaker & Co. series)
TAME A WILD HEART (Book 1, Tame series)
TAME A WILD WIND (Book 2, Tame series)
TAME A WILD BRIDE (Book 3, Tame series)
TAME A SUMMER HEART (short story, Tame series)
TAME A HONEYMOON HEART (novella, Tame series)

WEBSITE – www.cynthiawoolf.com

NEWSLETTER - http://bit.ly/1qBWhFQ